CARVED IN WOOD

BOOK 6 OF THE ART OF LOVE SERIES

DONNA MCDONALD

WWW.DONNAMCDONALDAUTHOR.COM

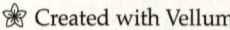 Created with Vellum

ACKNOWLEDGMENTS

Thanks to my husband, Bruce, for his constant love and understanding of what it is like to have to write when the urge hits. You are truly a hero to me.

Thanks to AJ for reading and for the feedback and for keeping my head in the right place to say what I wanted to say. Thank you. Thank you. Thank you.

DEDICATION

This book is for all the fans of the Art of Love series.

BOOK DESCRIPTION

He's obsessed with his art and with a woman who doesn't want to love him.

Maybe he should be grateful. Without the constant frustration, Joseph McEldowney figures he might never have answered any artistic urge to express his emotions. Now carving life from wood is all that soothes him. Too bad he can't carve out a place in this world where nothing matters except the heaven-sent pull he and Jillian Lansing have towards each other. She says he doesn't fit her long-term plans. If that's true, why should he torture himself with the short-term pleasure she's offering? But how can he turn her away when he can't get her off his mind? He loves her.

Jillian Lansing has been ambitious all her life. Despite helping care for her deceased brother's children, she kept all her own big dreams and plans for a family of her own. Sure, they've been put on hold for the last few years, but her life is way more stable now. Her auntie duties are relaxing into something almost normal. Reesa and Shane are doing great with the kids, and now expecting one of their own.Her lifelong best friend's pregnancy is another wake-up call for her. Despite both of them grieving the loss of their siblings, Reesa managed to find her perfect partner. So where is Jillian's? She's certainly dated enough trying to find him. And no, he definitely isn't Joseph.

"YOU'RE THIRTY-FIVE THIS YEAR, RIGHT?" THE DOCTOR ASKED.

Jillian nodded as she bit her lip. Why was it that bad news always seemed to start with someone pointing out your age. Getting older sucked. "The fibroids are still there, aren't they?"

"Yes. They're still there, but they haven't grown much. And the good news is that there are a lot of new drugs on the market. Sometimes they can help keep fibroids small but no medicine gets rid of them. That's still the case."

"Are we talking surgery to eventually remove them?" Jillian asked. She bit her lip when her doctor shifted in his chair.

"The problem with surgery is the location of the fibroids which might necessitate the removal of at least one ovary. The problem with the drugs is that they can affect fertility. Surgery to remove the fibroids will be our *only* option at some point. I would say if you're planning to have a family, you will need to do it this year, or at least by next year."

Jillian sighed at the news. After a few years of fighting her birth control, the reality of what her doctor was saying didn't surprise her, but it did depress her. "There's no serious man in my life right now, so I don't see myself having babies in the next year or even two."

"That doesn't have to stop you. If you're interested in alternatives, I highly recommend the Bluegrass Fertility Center here in Lexington. You can choose the perfect donor and they'll ship the sperm to my office for the procedure. If you don't find the diversity of donors you need there, there's another good service in Louisville. Shop until you find a donor match that suits you."

Shaking her head, Jillian lowered her gaze to stare at her bare feet. "I don't want children that badly. I've been helping raise my nieces and nephews since my brother and his wife died. They live with their other aunt. Honestly, my biological clock stops ticking after a day spent with them. They're a handful."

The doctor laughed and nodded. "I hear you. I have three of my own and children are a lot of work. You can let me know if you change your mind and I'll write a recommendation for you then. Let's see you back here in three months so we check everything again. If you start feeling a lot of pain, come in immediately. I want to keep close tabs on those fibroids."

"Sounds like a plan," Jillian said, smiling so he'd believe her. It actually sounded awful, but she was not having a meltdown in front of her OB-GYN.

When the exam room door closed behind him and the nurse that had been with him, Jillian slid off the table and pulled the paper gown from her body. She looked down at herself and frowned. All her life she'd been proud of her body and how she looked. She'd been proud of her curves and her smooth chocolate skin. Now she felt betrayed by it. On the outside everything was the same as always, but on the inside? Nothing was what it seemed.

That went double for the state of her hurting heart.

"THE NEW MINISTER IS SINGLE. I DON'T THINK HE'S COOKED A single meal for himself since he got here. We're having him over next week, so don't be making other plans for next Thursday night. And no working late either, Jillian."

"I already met the man," Jillian said to her mother, giving her a narrowed-eyed look. "He's got gray hair and has to be at least fifty. Why are you trying to hook me up with him?"

"If you weren't so particular, there might be some younger ones left to pick from. You can't be waiting until you're in your forties to have children. Lots of women start the change after forty-five."

"That's a whole decade away…" Jillian protested, shaking her head. "No fifty year old man is going to want to give me babies. I don't like older men anyway. Even if I had a child with someone like that, I'd end up taking care of the child and him as he got older. Is that really the life you want for me? Who's going to take care of you and Daddy?"

"More family might not seem so bad to you if you weren't always looking after…"

"Stop right there." Jillian's head snapped up as she threw out her hand. "I am doing what my brother would have wanted and what I think is right. I'm not arguing about it again."

"You're only helping out so much because that woman can't handle raising a family on her own. She should never have agreed to do it if it was that much of a struggle for her."

"That woman's name is Reesa, which you managed to call her all the years we were friends and growing up together. I'm sorry my best friend in the world is not the proper color you think she should be, but I'm leaving if you start putting her down. Reesa gave up everything for those children. She gave up a man, her work, her car—everything—and she did it to keep those children together as a family. You ought to be singing her praises for being such a saint. With all the traveling I did with my job, I could never have done it."

"Now you know we don't agree on her raising all the children. Your father and I both think her financial struggles are just the natural result of her stubbornness. She could have let us raise Zachary and Chelsea. She didn't have to be a martyr and do it all."

"Reesa was never going to let anyone further divide her home which had already been divided by more death and loss than most families have to endure in three or four generations," Jillian added. "I side with Reesa on all the actions she took to get custody of the children. I always will. I'm sorry—but that's the God's truth, Mama."

"You always talk like your father and I are bad people who would have kept Zack and Chelsea from seeing Brian and Sarah. That's an awful thing to think about your parents."

"You never offered to take all four of them. You only wanted two. That wasn't fair to them."

"It's called being realistic. We couldn't afford all four of them. The younger two still need a lot of attention and care. We travel far too much for all those counseling sessions and special classes she has them taking. The older two would have taken care of themselves."

Jillian frowned as she rolled her eyes. "Reesa and Shane haven't asked you and Daddy for anything. They let the children come visit you two guilt free. You should be grateful they don't hold a grudge over you dragging them through court. What you did already made the kids mad at you. How do you think they feel knowing you and Daddy only wanted two of them?"

"Why are you so defensive about this, Jillian? They're not

your children. They're not your responsibility. It was proper for the courts to decide and they did. Now we're all living with that decision whether it's for the greater good or not."

Jillian glanced away from her mother as she thought about how to answer without being meaner than she was already being. "No, they're not my children, but I'm sharing the responsibility for them as best I can. Reesa is like a sister to me and those children are my family. Plus, they may be the only mothering I ever do in my life."

"Well, if you weren't always pushing away good men..."

"Like the one you set me up with last month who wanted me to do his laundry and take care of his house while he was out of town?"

"It wasn't like he was asking for the world, Jillian. His mother was too sick to do it."

"Mama, we had two dates. We were still practically strangers. You don't ask a woman after two dates to mind your house and wash your damn clothes."

"You look for any excuse. No man's perfect, Jillian."

Jillian sighed and stood. She picked up her coffee cup and snack plate. "A woman has a right to be loved. If I can't have that, then I'd rather live alone."

"Love isn't all that wonderful, girl. Love can lead a good woman down paths she shouldn't be walking. Look around at all the people you know getting divorced and tell me that's not true."

Jillian watched her mother squirm. With role models like her ambivalent parents, it was a miracle her brother had fallen in love and married before he was twenty. Oh, how often she'd wished that she'd been as lucky. If she had, she would have had someone in her life all this time.

"That's a pretty jaded view of love, Mama. Are you saying you don't love Daddy?"

"Of course, I love your father. He's a good man and a good provider. He's given me a life I wouldn't have had without him. He gave you and your brother a good life."

"A life where he was gone all the time. He wasn't there for Jackson and he wasn't there for me. You were the only one who came to anything we did in school. We grew up without Daddy making any contribution to what we did. He can't make up the difference by being in Zack's life."

"How can you be so ungrateful? Your father gave you a life where you never wanted for anything."

Except parental love and approval, Jillian thought, but didn't say it aloud. Her mother hadn't married for love and didn't seem to regret that she hadn't. The woman who gave her life would never understand that the only real need Jillian had in the whole world was to be wanted and adored.

"I appreciate all you and Daddy did to raise me. I'm not ungrateful one bit, but the older I get the more I know that I can't live the life you think I should. I hope one day you can understand that I need different things. Having a husband is not even a goal for me. Finding love is."

"All you're going to find is a broken heart at the end of your hopes, Jillian. You're thirty-five. It's time to be practical. You don't want to grow old alone. No one has to be a maiden aunt these days."

Jillian headed to the kitchen with her dishes. "I don't intend to be one, but if that's how life works out for me, so be it. I'm not going to settle."

2

JOSEPH STOPPED SANDING WHEN HE HEARD THE DOORBELL RING. HE thought about ignoring it for a moment, but changed his mind. His obsession with what he was doing wasn't healthy—he knew that from confessing his frustration to his smart-ass psychologist friend—so any kind of interruption had to be the universe intervening. Right?

Rolling his eyes, Joe groaned. Now he was even starting to sound like Shane. His best friend from childhood had gotten a job at a research university and Joe had been a Larson lab rat ever since. If he didn't love Shane like a brother, he'd go over to his house and kick his giant Larson ass for planting so much worry in his brain.

So what if he'd cleaned out the spare bedroom in his apartment and converted it into a work space for a hobby? Using a whole room for it didn't mean he was going crazy. Not long ago, his projects had been spread out across the dining room, but he'd outgrown the space. And okay--he'd wanted to hide it from himself to slow his compulsive need to finish it which often meant working until two in the morning.

Blowing out a breath, Joe set the sandpaper next to the base of the mahogany statue he was polishing and closed the bedroom door behind him as he left the room. His need to hide what he was doing was instinctual… and strong.

He didn't buy all the woo-woo his Larson buddy did, but his Irish ancestors had definitely passed down an urge to trust his gut.

"Stop knocking already. I'm coming," he yelled.

Expecting the now escalating pounding to be someone's lost pizza delivery, Joe opened the door and glared. But it wasn't a pizza delivery gone astray. It was the last person he'd expected to ever see standing outside his home. Joe stared and blinked his blue eyes—totally at a loss for anything clever.

"Are you going stare at me all night or invite me in?" she demanded.

Words returned when he heard her snarky demand. "I think my brain is still working out whether or not you're a mirage. Why are you here, Jillian? I thought you didn't want anything to do with me. Wasn't that what you said the last time we spoke?"

Joe watched as she bit her lip and dropped her chocolate gaze. He followed the downward motion and they both ended up staring at her pointy red shoes with heels that made her his height. His eyes wouldn't stay down though and instead traveled up her shapely legs and over her knees to where her snug red dress hugged the curves of her ample hips. He wanted under that stretchy red fabric almost more than he wanted to breathe, but it was never going to happen. It wasn't what Jillian wanted. And he'd already pushed their attraction farther than she'd ever wanted to take it.

He ran a hand through his hair. He should say something ugly and run Jillian off once and for all. That was the model his old man had set for him. Insults had flown between his parents and his father had gotten meaner and meaner with the passage of time. If his father had ever smacked his mother around, Joe hadn't seen it happen, but it had been a constant concern for him, even as a child. He'd worried about it until the day he'd come home from school and seen Will Larson talking nose-to-nose with his father. Two days afterward his father had packed up and left.

"You haven't answered any of my questions," Joe said, stalling while he decided what to do about her. The last time he'd talked to Jillian was four months ago, and before that, it had been at Shane and Reesa's wedding. Dwelling on that Larson fiasco led to a madness that neither drink nor other women had been able to rid him of.

"I know," Jillian said, shifting on her heels. "I don't have any answers. I just..." Her eyes closed on a resigned sigh. "I went to dinner tonight—on a date—and I..." Her gaze opened and sought his. "I was thinking of you instead of him. It seemed rude to keep doing that."

Joe chuckled. "You're right. That was rude. But it's still no answer."

"Making me stand out here in your hallway and confess my sins isn't an answer either. The only thing I can say is that I'm obsessed with you and I want to get over it. That's why I'm here."

Joe crossed his arms and leaned against the door jam. "You're mistaking me for Shane. I'm not a therapist... nor am I a monk. If you come through my door, I can't promise you anything is going to go the way you're probably spinning it in your head."

Jillian nodded. "I'm not looking for promises. In fact, I'm not looking for anything but some peace of mind."

"See? That's where you and I disagree, Jillian. I think you're looking for something more than you're willing to admit to yourself... or to me. And I think I know exactly what you're looking for, but a man has to have some pride."

Jillian snorted. "If you wanted to keep your secrets to yourself, Joseph, you should have worn tighter pants."

Joe grunted and shrugged. "If you'd wanted something uncomplicated, you should have gone home with your dinner date." He pointed at her and then at his own chest. "We—you and I—are complicated. We always have been."

Jillian grunted back. "We are *not* complicated. We're just obsessed."

"Well, I can agree with that, but I'm still not sure I want to let you in. That dress you're wearing is like a weapon. I'm thoroughly threatened by my reaction to it."

"Yeah, well, I'm not sure I want to let you in either, but I'm here to see if you're still interested." Jillian sighed and then shook her head. "I'm sorry for the bad pun—it was all I could think of."

Irritated that Joseph hadn't thrown the door wide the moment she'd shown up, Jillian crossed her arms to mirror his resistant stance. She was an ample woman all over and the action made the front of her dress slide down her cleavage. It made Joe's gaze slide down as well and her girls warmed with remembering his eager mouth on them. Damn it.

Once again she asked herself "Why him?" and once again there was no reasonable answer to that query. Joseph McEldowney was not the one for her. Joe was just... Joe. He was shaggy Shane Larson's childhood friend and definitely did not fit her plans. She couldn't—wouldn't—let her mother and father down this hard, despite her disappointment in their viewpoints. Her parents were finally getting used to Reesa and Shane having custody of her nieces and nephews—at least a little. The family boat had already been rocked as hard as it could without overturning.

To say her parents didn't understand that her bigger, more inclusive worldview was an understatement. All the luxury they lived in and all the comfort they had earned hadn't sweetened the bitterness of what they still saw as their dead son's defection in his choice of a wife. Color preference was only one aspect of their judgment. They hadn't approved of Reesa's sister or Reesa. Reesa's family had been naturally wealthy and eccentric enough to adopt Reesa. Her bootstrap to wealthy parents thought they'd earned their right to their snooty attitude as well as their money.

It was all just craziness because her brother had created exactly the kind of loving family he'd wanted. Jackson had worked hard on being a great father and husband. Instead of an NBA career, he'd taken a coaching job to avoid being away from his wife and children. Her parents' dream of having a famous NBA player son hadn't died quietly. They'd blamed her sister-in-law—Reesa's sweet sister—and her lack of career for her brother's choices.

Despite her own financial success, which was starting to be as good as her father's, Jillian hadn't made them proud of her yet either. She'd dated plenty of men but had never come close to finding one she cared enough about to spend her life with. Color aside… coming here to sleep with a man who'd forsaken his engineering degree to work as a handyman carpenter would surely be one more mark in the disappointment column.

Jillian sighed. Her situation with Joseph McEldowney was a no win situation. She couldn't take this obsession seriously— beyond needing to indulge it in order to move past it. Being celibate had never suited her, but she'd been unable to feel desire for anyone else since she'd kissed the man still staring at her.

She needed to get Joseph out of her system and move on— and the sooner the better.

"Are you letting me in or not?" Jillian asked.

"Yeah. I guess I am," Joe said with resignation. "I'll order a pizza. I haven't eaten and you must be starved."

"Why would you say that? I just told you I was at dinner before I came here," Jillian protested.

Joe snorted. "And you probably pretended to eat. I know how women are on dates, especially if this was a new guy."

"We go to the same nightclubs. I know all about how you date," Jillian grumbled.

Joe swung back and stepped into her. He kissed her hard, his mouth mercilessly taking all the liberties it wanted. His muscles tightened when Jillian moaned and his heart beat faster when her arms wove themselves around his waist. He dragged his mouth away and put his forehead on hers. "I haven't been with anyone since Shane's freaking wedding and it's all your fault. No one smells like you or tastes like you or kisses like you…"

"Stop… just stop saying that shit…" Jillian ordered, her palm shoving against a strong shoulder that she knew had gotten that way from hours and hours of hard manual labor. She doubted Joe had ever seen the inside of a gym.

"Are you afraid of the truth?" Joe demanded.

"Yes," Jillian confessed, returning his blue-eyed glare. "And of you."

Joe nodded and let her go. "Well, I'm afraid of you too. Guess that makes us even. You can stay for pizza… or the whole evening. Your call."

"You sound like you don't care one way or the other," Jillian said, crossing her arms again—this time to hug herself. His words were honest. They shouldn't have hurt. So why did they?

"You coming here means everything to me, but I'm smart enough to know we're not on the same page," Joe said softly.

"That makes letting you stay one of the dumbest mistakes I could ever make."

"But you're still going to make it?"

Joe smiled as he nodded. "Yeah. I'm still going to make it."

He tugged her inside and closed the door on the rest of the world.

3

"Woman, you look ready to pop at seven months. That's what you get for bedding that big old shaggy Viking you married," Jillian teased as she sat down on the couch next to the basket of laundry waiting to be folded.

The baby was estimated to be nine pounds already and Reesa had nearly two months to go. A C-section was in her friend's future and Jillian knew Reesa was trying hard to make peace with it. Whether boy or girl—something Reesa and Shane had decided not to learn in advance—their child was already proving that he or she intended to take after its giant father.

"I don't want to talk about the state of my body at the moment. Let's talk about something more fun. How was your date?" Reesa asked, as she lowered herself into a chair.

Jillian didn't look up at her very pregnant friend as she folded towels. "My date was boring, just like they all are lately. You can tell what a guy thinks of you from the restaurant he picks. Last night my date took me to a sushi place even though I told him I didn't like sushi. He apparently loves the stuff."

"Did you starve while he ate?" Reesa asked.

Jillian shook her head. "No. I had some miso soup and a small salad. Then I went..." she paused and sighed. "After the date ended, I had three slices of pizza to drown my misery."

Reesa chuckled. "Another bad date bites the dust. You can't hang with a man who won't feed you. What is with cheap-ass guys these days?"

Wanting to avoid all thoughts of pizza and the generous man who'd eaten the rest of what she hadn't, Jillian pointed at the three baskets of clothes. "What's next to fold?"

"Just the one that says Princess Sarah on it. Brian and Chelsea take care of their own these days. I wash and dry. Everyone folds their own."

"About damn time," Jillian said firmly. "You're not their laundry maid."

Reesa laughed at Jillian's tone. "Are you kidding? I'm living large these days. I'm suddenly getting help in the kitchen too."

"How? Chelsea takes after me. She hates anything to do with that room. Is Brian learning to cook?"

Reesa laughed. "No, but he loads the dishwasher without complaint. That's all the progress I can hope for from a thirteen year old boy."

"So who's helping with cooking?"

"This is Chelsea's senior year. She's trying to convince us that she's mature enough to live with a girlfriend when she goes to college. She doesn't want to live in a dorm."

Jillian chuckled. "Smart girl. Has she gotten over her crush on Brandon Barrymore yet?"

Reesa shook her head. "I don't think so, but they're very low key with each other—very discreet. Sometimes I think they're more friends than actually dating. I do catch them holding hands once in a while, but she makes him keep his distance around family."

"Good for her. I talked to her about setting boundaries. A woman has got to have some respect for herself."

Reesa sighed and shook her head. "I've worried plenty about feeding them, but I've got to say that I've never once worried about their moral decisions. And I've definitely not worried about Chelsea since Brandon rescued her from that frat guy."

"Lots of women end up learning that lesson the hard way. Trying to convert the bad boys is a bad-bad habit to get into."

"I want to agree, but you know I thought Shane was a bad boy. I can't criticize anyone when I had that habit myself."

Jillian laughed at Reesa's honesty. "Yeah, but Shane only looks tough. Inside, he's about as good-hearted as men get. Sometimes Shane reminds me of Jackson. My brother acted tough around everyone except your sister. It didn't take long after he met April for him to drop that male bravado act."

"They were so great together. The kids they made are great too," Reesa said, smiling softly. "Losing their parents affected Chelsea and Zack the most. They seemed nearly grown-up when I moved in with them full-time. Now Brian? That boy is wicked and sneaky, not to mention an absolute delight when he turns on the charm. He's going to be a problem as he gets older —you can bet on it."

Jillian grinned in agreement. "Oh, I'm sure you and your shaggy Viking with his psychology degree can handle one smart-ass teenage boy with raging hormones."

Reesa laughed. "I don't know, Jillian. Brian's so much like Jackson that it makes my heart hurt. And I remember my sister falling hard for him the first time he spoke to her." She sighed over the future. "I hope Brian waits a good long time before falling in love."

"No wonder you're so worried about adding a brand new child to your crazy household. Raising kids is overwhelming."

"You know it," Reesa said honestly, sighing again at her worry. "Having this baby is going to be fine though—or mostly fine. Shane is great with children, but I'm... well, I'm still adjusting to the ones I inherited. And Princess Sarah is still very needy. Now I'm going to be asking her to share my attention with a baby. So yeah... I'm a bit worried."

Jillian huffed. "Well, let those worries go, girlfriend. I've got your back. Now that they hired me for the director's job, I'm going to be handling marketing and social media instead of jetting all over the world to check product quality. It'll still be long work hours for me, but I'll be able to be here more."

"Jillian, I love you for wanting to help us, but you need to find your own life. Your financial help made my life with the children possible. Now Shane makes enough money to care for all of us. I can even hire household help if I need it—and baby help too. Carrie's delivering the art gallery's records to the house so I'm not even going to miss my own work. All is well with me and the kids. Seriously—it's time for you to focus on yourself."

"What about their college tuition?" Jillian asked.

"Zack's got a full-ride basketball scholarship and his grades are good. Chelsea's working on weekends and saving her money. Plus, Shane has signed up for a program to get half of Chelsea's tuition paid if she goes to UK. If she gets scholarships too, then Chelsea can use her savings to live with her friend like she wants. Chelsea's going to be fine."

"Okay. How about the other two? Brian's only got a few years until he'll be needing help with college."

Reesa shook her head. "Unless something miraculous happens to change his mind, Brian is going to art school. Jessica and Michael are working with him every week. Who knows how far they'll take his art? I don't know how we'll pay for his formal training yet, but we'll find a way. Then we'll have a good long while before Princess Sara gets old enough for college."

"No worries about the little princess. I'll be paying for fashion school for her," Jillian joked as usual. "That girl has a sharp eye."

"And a smart mouth..." Reesa added, grinning when she made Jillian laugh. "We are the best aunts in the world, aren't we?"

"We definitely are. I regret nothing about what we've done. I hope you don't either," Jillian said.

"You know I don't. This is my family—*our* family. Just think, by the time Sarah goes to college, any babies we have could be right behind her."

"Those baby hormones are making you delirious," Jillian exclaimed, chuckling over the idea. "I'm certainly not going to be getting a child from anything I've been doing lately."

"Why? All your dates can't be as bad as the sushi guy."

"That's what you think," Jillian said firmly. She pushed the basket away. "The only sex I'm having at the moment is..." She froze and stared at Reesa who arched an eyebrow. Wow—the truth had almost slipped out on its own.

"The only sex you're having is with yourself?" Reesa finished with a laugh.

"No. I'm not that desperate yet," Jillian said, unable to lie completely. "I have a guy that I..."

"You have a booty call guy?" Reesa filled in with a giggle.

"Something like that."

"Is he good?" Reesa asked.

"I don't know," Jillian said with a frown. "We haven't got that far."

"Maybe you need to talk to him about the definition of a booty call."

"Shut up," Jillian ordered, snorting as Reesa dissolved into giggles. "We're doing other things."

"Other things?" Reesa repeated as she laughed harder.

"Yes, smart-ass... *other things*."

"Good other things?" Reesa asked with a grin. "Geez... this sounds like high school. I hated high school."

Jillian sighed. She had never, ever, ever been able to lie to the petite woman grilling her. Not since they were six. But she was not about to confess what she had yet to understand. "Let's just say the man is the best at everything we've done so far... and yes, it feels a bit like having a high school boyfriend. The man is creative about providing me relief. But no, it's not all I want from him. However, it's better than going without or resorting to toys."

"So why don't you date the creative, sex guy?"

Jillian looked away. "I can't. He's not my type."

"Why? No chocolate?"

Snorting, Jillian didn't raise her head. "You think you know everything about me, don't you?"

"I know you avoid dating men who don't have skin as dark as yours. I keep hoping you'll realize that's about your parents and not about you. Plus, you haven't brought a single guy to meet me. I've been worried about you for years."

"Did it ever occur to you that I've moved beyond all the one-night stands and flings? Dating the creative, sexy guy would be an act of futility. He has nothing going for him that's on my long-term list. When I meet the *right* man, the creative, sexy guy will become history."

"Except he's obviously talented at *other things* that maybe aren't on your long-term list either. If he makes you laugh, you're in big trouble, Jillian. That's how they get you. The sex is just how they seal the deal."

Jillian rolled her eyes. "He bought me pizza and we made

out on his couch like horny teenagers. I went home several hours later with my underwear shoved into my purse. It was not a proud moment for me. I haven't done anything like that since college."

Reesa laughed. "If he's that talented, when are you going back to get the real thing from him?"

Jillian picked up a pillow and threw it at her friend. "As soon as I can. Are you satisfied?"

"Why yes, I am. Shane takes great care of my needs, but I thought we were talking about you."

"Oh—haha. The shaggy Viking is good in bed. I knew that the day I picked him out for you. He walked you out with his fingers on your back. The man was a toucher and those are the best kind in bed."

"I'm sure you'll find an equally perfect man eventually. You have latent talent in that area."

"My pickup mojo doesn't work as well for me," Jillian said with a sigh. "I can't seem to find any guy that has it all."

"Maybe because none of them do, Jillian," Reesa said firmly, pushing her whale form out of the chair. "Put being good in bed and loving you outside of it at the top of that list of yours. All the other stuff can be worked out. Jobs and titles and the rest come and go with fate."

"OMG, I thought I'd never live long enough to hear you talk this way. The realist has become an optimist. It must be those pregnancy hormones," Jillian teased.

"Love can change your life in ways you can't even imagine until it happens to you," Reesa said. "Want some cherry pie? I think I might even have some ice cream to go on it. Shane's been doing the shopping. I'm getting spoiled."

"Sounds like you have your husband trained. What's your secret?"

"Sex is a very powerful thing, Jillian. Very powerful."

"I hear you, girlfriend. I hear you," Jillian said, laughing as she followed her tiny, pregnant friend into the kitchen.

4

JOE LAUGHED WHEN WILL WALKED INTO THE HOUSE COVERED IN white dust. The only clean spot on the man was around his nose and mouth where he'd worn a protective mask.

"Good thing Jessica isn't here to see you dumping all that mess on her kitchen floor."

"Grinding down the stone is the messiest part of my process. That's why we had you install the extra sliding door in the dining area. The mess is way easier to clean up from the tile. And by the way," Will said as he pointed to what Joe was working on. "I am loving not having that wall there. I can see the whole kitchen now. Taking it down was a great suggestion."

Joe nodded. "Yeah, I knew it would look better. Today was the hardest part of your renovation. Opening the kitchen to the living room will be a lot easier."

"Can't wait to see that too. Excuse me a minute."

Joe watched Will carefully roll the snug dust-covered t-shirt up his chest and over his head. Despite being in his fifties, Will had arm and chest muscles as well defined as his sons. All the

Larson males were built like that. Joe envied them their genes. He grinned at Will.

"I hope I look as fit as you do when I get to be your age. My father's put on thirty pounds, gotten soft around the middle, and looks two decades older than he should. Since I look so much like him, his appearance worries me."

Will used the clean inside of his shirt to wipe the dust from his face. "Your muscles will definitely stay toned if you keep doing what you're doing for a living. Keeping fit is always hard work—in a gym or out of it. I have to lift a few weights now and again to keep in good enough shape to do what I do. My art has always provided all the motivation I need."

Joe lifted his nail gun over his head and shot a couple of nails into the new header. "Guess I'm lucky that I like hard work. What I do for a living keeps the bills paid, lets me work on my clock, and it's satisfying. Since I paid for my own college degree, I have no guilt at all about not signing on with some engineering firm when I graduated. My internship was enough to show me how restrictive and demanding that kind of career would have been."

Will snorted. "You hung around the boys and me far too much to grow up and do something typical for a living."

"That's probably true. Plus, Shane's the least normal of you all. He corrupted me when we were eight. He drew all the kids in our class as superheroes. That's still the most awesome thing I've ever seen anyone do. Shane astounds me with what he's accomplished, especially since we're not even thirty yet."

Will chuckled at Joe's fondness for his youngest. They were as tight as brothers--always had been. "Shane is an anomaly. Even I don't understand how he's managed to get so much done. Most of us walk a more curvy path to our destinies, and speaking of destinies, did you bring your latest project with you? I'm excited to take a look at it."

Joe lowered the nail gun as he reluctantly nodded. "I did bring it, but I'm having second thoughts now. I appreciate all the pointers you've passed along, but it just hit me that what I've done is going to seem like a kid's popsicle art to you."

Will grinned as he shook his head. "Doesn't matter if it does, Joseph. You have to start somewhere. Let me wash up and put on a clean shirt. We'll have coffee and take a break—if that's okay?"

"I have someplace else to be this afternoon anyway, but I promise I'll get back to this tomorrow." Joe sighed in resignation. "You'll just call me a coward now if I don't let you see it, won't you?"

"I will chant it over and over until you cave," Will said firmly.

Sighing louder, Joe bent and set the nail gun on the floor. "Fine. Let me get it from the truck."

HE'D TURNED DOWN WILL'S OFFER OF COFFEE AND SETTLED FOR the bottle of water he'd stashed in his lunch cooler. His stomach was unsettled, and he couldn't sit still while Will inspected what he'd done. If this gut-wrenching worry over being judged was what being an artist was like, he likely wasn't cut out to be one. Watching Will's silent inspection was making him ill.

Will's cool assessing glare gave nothing away—one of the many reasons William Larson had been such an effective school principal.

He should have just let Will pay him to remove that wall separating the dining room from the kitchen instead of bargaining his labor in exchange for lessons and tips. Carving was a hobby for him—not a profession.

"How long did this take you?"

Joe lifted both shoulders. "About a week to get the basic shape. It took another week to get the details right. I painted and gel stained it so you could get a feel for what I'm envisioning the finished product to look like. I think if I put a couple more days into polishing it I can further improve the texture of its skin."

Will nodded and set the wooden rhino on the table. "The detail on the eyes is amazing. Is this the first piece you've finished?"

Joe grunted. "No. I've finished five others, but they're definitely kindergarten level. This one turned out better than I expected. If you set it on a shelf across the room, the eyes will seem to follow you."

"How did you get that to work?"

Adjusting his body in the chair, Joe lifted both shoulders again. "I'm not completely sure, but I think it's the way I do the eyes. They look round, but if you look super close, you'll see they're actually a hexagon. I thought that would give them more depth."

"It probably gives them a 3-D effect," William said.

Joe nodded. "Yeah. That was my hope."

Will picked up his coffee. "Well, your hope has been realized. It worked out just like you planned."

"Really?" Joe asked, clearing his throat when he all but squeaked his surprise.

Nodding, Will sipped his perfect brew. "The feet need more attention. You rushed those. Sometimes you have to step away from a piece and then go back to it. That allows you to see it with fresh eyes. Working obsessively you can often miss what it needs to get to the next level. Your rhino is unique and very striking from the shoulders up. The feet are your next level."

Joe swallowed hard before answering. "The pictures I found in my research didn't zoom in close enough for me to see the details of the feet. All people seem to want to see of a rhino is his face and horn."

One side of Will's mouth lifted in a smirk. "Visit the Cincinnati zoo, Joseph. Take your own pictures. Use the zoom on your phone camera to get the detail."

Joe grinned at the simplicity of the advice. "Yeah. That would probably work."

"Do it soon," Will ordered as he grinned back. "Can I keep the rhino for a little while? There's someone I want to show it to. Wood's not my natural medium and I don't want to steer you wrong. I'll take good care of it. You can have it back in a few days."

"Keep it. I'll make another one. Just please don't tell anyone it's mine," Joe said.

Will chuckled as his head swung side-to-side. "No. I don't want it like this. The feet aren't finished. I'm going to give it back and you're going to fix his feet. You'll thank me later."

Joe grunted and gave him a sheepish look. "Okay. Sure. But you mostly like it?"

Will nodded. "Not just mostly... I *really* like it. Do you like it?"

Joe picked up the rhino and turned it around to inspect it again. "Carving this was nearly as much fun as knocking down your wall was. I guess my answer is yes. I like it."

"Congratulations," Will said, rising to take his coffee cup to the sink. "You're now an artist. Liking your own work is the hardest part."

Joe wasn't sure he agreed with that assessment, but he liked the idea of being called an artist, especially by someone as talented as Will Larson.

STILL DWELLING ON ALL WILL SAID ABOUT HIS CARVING, JOE LEFT at two-thirty and headed downtown. It took him forever to find a parking place for the truck, but he finally did. At nearly three-thirty, he pushed through the door of the building and entered an oasis of calm, despite the bickering people in the middle of the floor.

Across the room, the pedestals he'd made for Carrie last month were lined up against the wall, except for the two that she'd moved out to the main floor. She had asked for varying heights and for the stands to be painted black. Her directions had been precise and easy enough to follow.

He'd turned the pedestals from huge blocks of wood using his storage locker setup. One day he'd like to have a garage or an actual workshop. First, though, he'd have to buy a house. His savings wasn't quite enough for a down payment yet, but perhaps in another year.

Carrie was really busy. It looked like she was setting up some sort of mixed media art show. She, Drake, and what appeared to be several college students, were busy hanging framed art and arranging something in cases. Joe couldn't see what it was. He wondered what was going on the pedestals. It had to be something significant—some larger piece that would draw more than just an admiring eye or two.

He shoved his hands in his pockets as he moved forward to talk to her. "Now I see why you need a rolling wall. You want to use it for these larger framed pieces."

"Exactly," Carrie said, stepping away to smile. "Hi, Joe. What brings you here so soon? I thought you were going to wait for me to send some measurements."

Joe lifted one shoulder. "I was. Then I got the urge to visit."

"That's great," Carrie said, putting her hand on his arm. "Get the urge this weekend too. The gallery is hosting our first art show for the place where I used to work. It's a mixed media showcase. We have a little of everything."

Joe nodded politely. "Sure. It looks like you're busy—probably too busy to talk to me."

"I'm busy, but as you can see, I have a lot of help. A break won't kill me. Besides, Drake is nearly as good as I am when it comes to setting up the framed art. What's a movable wall going to cost me?"

Joe shrugged as they walked away from the group. "It depends on how big you want it and what it's going to take to make it. When I figure it out, I'll email you an estimate."

"Be gentle with me," Carrie said with a laugh.

"I always am with beautiful women," Joe replied.

Carrie giggled at his mild flirting. "Your gift of flattery must come from your Irish ancestors."

Joe grinned. "You'd think that was the case, but the truth is that I learned everything I know from Shane Larson. He was always the master of knowing exactly what to say to women." He looked around the space. "How often do you change your offerings in here?"

"Frequently. I only take in art pieces that I honestly believe I can sell. When I move a certain number of them, I go looking for more," Carrie motioned for Joe to follow her. "Come look at a piece that's not for sale. It's the only one of its kind in the gallery."

Joe trailed after her until Carrie stopped in front of a carving that she was keeping inside a glass case. He inspected it instinctively—his mind already critiquing how the artist hadn't done all that he could have to it. Was this what Will meant? That you could see what needed to be done if you had the right perspective?

Joe lifted his chin at the piece. "What kind of art is this considered?"

"African art," Carrie said. "I've seen better craftsmanship, but this was the only reasonably priced piece I could find when I went looking for some to buy. When African art got popular, representation of tribal life started being mass produced in factories. Real African art always ends up in the bigger galleries. I bought this piece out of desperation to add some cultural diversity to the gallery's catalog. I'm sure it would sell to someone, but I'm not putting a price on it until I get a lead on a wider collection of pieces."

"It's a good piece, just looks like whoever made it rushed doing the man's body. The face is great."

Carrie lifted an eyebrow and turned to stare. "That's exactly what happened. You have a good eye for detail."

Joe lifted a shoulder. "I work with wood all the time. You have to be patient with it to get it to become what you want it to be. I used to make furniture as a side gig. I have a great appreciation for what it takes to turn wood into something beautiful."

"Do you enjoy this kind of art?" Carrie asked, her gaze turning toward the case again.

Joe nodded. "I suppose I favor sculpture and like it better than most others. I'm not into abstract art although I do like some of Michael's newer pieces. On the whole, I prefer seeing reality reflected. This artist does give me a sense of what the shepherd's everyday life is like. The details of his face show the pride he has. The details on each animal show the artist's true skill. He just rushed carving the body."

Carrie grinned at Joe's very accurate assessment. "I'd love to do a whole show of African art. My chances aren't great of finding someone willing to show their work in my small gallery."

"I'd love to see you do that too," Joe said, thinking such a showing would give him fresh inspiration and research from something other than the internet. "Any idea where I can find the nearest collection of real African art."

"I think the Museum of Fine Arts in Boston has the best collection," Carrie answered instantly.

Joe grunted. "Shane and I went to school up that way. I might just have to make that drive."

"If Ivy was a bit older, I'd offer to go with you. I'm still nursing at night."

"She's a cutie, Carrie. How's Michael adjusting to fatherhood?"

"No baby has ever been loved more. Stick around a bit. He may bring her by. They were out doing errands today. The man takes her everywhere with him."

"I would love to stay but I need to get home. My work is only half done. I got the wall down at Will and Jessica's. The kitchen and dining room are now completely open. Next up is an archway that will open the kitchen to the living room. I'm trying to finish up there."

"Sounds wonderful—I'd love to have a real dining room."

Joe smiled. "You'll have to talk your husband into letting me add on an extension in the back. We could make that happen if he'd given up a wee bit of his courtyard."

"Really?" Carrie asked.

Joe shrugged. "Don't turn those pleading eyes in my direction. I'll not be the one telling that to your husband. That's your job. I'm just the carpenter."

Carrie laughed. "Now I want to go home and take a look. How much of the courtyard?"

"Let's discuss it later. Want that moveable wall for here first?"

"I do," Carrie admitted. "I'll send you the measurements when I figure it out."

"Mind if I take a few of my own before I leave? I might be able to make a suggestion or two about size."

"Sure. Take your time, Joe. Hang out all you want. There are sodas in the break room refrigerator."

"Thanks," Joe said, admiring the energetic woman who quickly walked away.

Both Shane and Michael had married amazing women. He hoped one day to be that lucky as well.

5

WILL KNOCKED ON THE OFFICE DOOR AND PEERED INSIDE. "HELLO there, Professor James. Got a few minutes to talk to an old friend?"

The art professor lifted his head from his computer and smiled. "William Larson. I haven't seen you since you came to visit my class. When was that? Three years ago I believe. How's the beautiful Ellen doing?"

Will chuckled as he walked inside the office. "Ellen's married to someone else now and so am I. But it's all good— we're all good. The four of us get together for dinner. God, was that TMI? I'm starting to sound like my sons. What I'm trying to say is that things have worked out as they were meant to in my life and Ellen's."

"Good to hear it—all of it," Simba answered, waving his hand.

Will smiled. "Larson men are resilient."

Simba belly laughed. "I would have to agree, especially now that I have confirmed where Michael got his wicked side. I always suspected it was from you. My father would have killed me for doing even half of what Michael got by with while he was here. I might not have witnessed it, but his exploits are still legendary. He comes by now and again to visit the starving art students. He seems to enjoy the role of arrogant, local celebrity."

"I'm not blind to my son's flaws, but I had to stop apologizing for him years ago. It was too much work," Will said with a resigned sigh as Simba laughed. "Michael's married and a father now. He's become domesticated since you probably last saw him."

Simba snickered. "I joke with you, William. Your son has done a lot for a man his age. I should know because I'm not much older. And I greatly admire all Michael has accomplished with his art. In his career, I'm sure his notoriety serves him far better than my intelligence serves me in mine."

"That sounds bad, Simba. UK not treating you well?" Will asked with genuine concern.

"No, no. I love it here," Simba said with a head shake. "But teaching art is not the same as making it. I miss being in my own workshop. Grading is not the same as creating. There is no time for brooding until your fingers grow restless to paint. It is the downside of academia."

"You sound like my wife. Jessica was a high school art teacher when we met. Now she makes art and works at the gallery Michael and his wife own. Jessica says she's living her dream life. I tell myself it's because of me, but she'd just laugh if I said it aloud in front of her."

"Are you talking about the Jessica who works at the gallery? Jessica Daniels? *That's who you married?*"

Will's lips firmed. "Why do you ask? Did you date her?"

"*Did I date her?* Come on—you flatter me," Simba said with a full grin. "We're referring to the tall, gorgeous red-head who speaks her mind, right?"

Will nodded. "Yes. That's Jessica, alright. Her daughter married Drake Barrymore."

"I am aware. I was in Africa visiting my cousin and couldn't make the wedding. Their relationship sure happened fast."

"Things accelerated once Brooke got to talking to my boys."

"Drake is a fine man," Simba said.

Will nodded in agreement. "Yes, he is. Jessica and I are both happy to see our children in such great relationships."

"And the Barrymores are expecting a baby girl now, right? I know this only because I'm supposed to fill in while Drake's taking paternity leave."

"Filling in for the Chair of the UK Art Department? Not bad for a man your age, Dr. James."

Simba rolled his eyes. "Yes. You'd think that, wouldn't you? But when my family heard my boss was having a baby, I've heard nothing but complaining about my unwed status. I'm turning thirty-six this year and haven't produced the prerequisite grandchildren my parents expected me to by now. They do not care about my academic accomplishments. Where are the babies who are related to us? That is my parent's only question."

Will rubbed his nose as he fought not to laugh. "Well, Drake's over 50. You could always find yourself a younger wife and let nature take its course like he did."

Simba huffed. "I'm around children all day. When I date, I want someone close to my own age. Worse, I prefer my women to be interesting as well as beautiful. Such females are rare here in Lexington." He leaned back in his chair. "What brings you here today, Will? I assume it was not to discuss my miserable love life. I see an artistic gleam in your eyes."

Grinning at the astute guess, Will reached into his jacket pocket and pulled out the wooden rhino. He handed it to Simba over the desk.

"Nice piece," Simba said. "The artist didn't finish the feet."

Will laughed. "He's going to when I get the rhino back to him. I'm insisting."

"Looks a bit Ethiopian in design. The eyes are amazing. I'm guessing the artist is not one of our students or I'd already know his carving technique. Where does he study?"

Laughing, Will shrugged. "I suppose you could say he studies at the school of hard knocks."

"Your joking metaphor does not surprise me. Every artist has had an address there," Simba stated.

Will nodded in agreement and then smiled. "Would you believe my carpenter made that piece? Before this, all Joe's made is furniture. He said he got restless one day and started carving. Joe and Shane are best friends, so I've known the boy since he was six. Joe's extremely tight-lipped about his personal life but I think there's a woman involved in that restlessness."

"This piece is exceptional for a first timer. He's obviously a natural," Simba admitted as he studied the rhino more closely. "And his attention to detail is amazing. I think I'm jealous of his skill. I do not have this kind of eye. If I did, I would not be teaching. My work would be in all the museums."

"Thanks for looking at it. I needed a second opinion—a more educated opinion. Joe's new to this and wood's not my medium."

"Hard to believe he's working as a carpenter when he could be doing so much more. Perhaps such talent flows in the Kentucky water. I should drink more."

"For him, it's just a hobby. I've been trading critique sessions and carving lessons for house renovations," Will confessed.

Simba belly laughed at the story as he handed the rhino back. "Perhaps I should get a cut of that action for giving him my educated appraisal. I need some new bookshelves for my house. Tell him to come see me."

Will lowered his chin and thought hard for a moment. He lifted his face and smiled. "How about a lead on a hot date with a great woman instead? I think I know someone you'd like."

Simba shook a finger. "Now you're reminding me of Michael again."

Will lifted a shoulder. "I've had worse comparisons. You interested or not?"

Simba lifted a hand and sighed loudly. "I suppose I am since I'm still listening."

"There's a multi-media show at the gallery Saturday night. Jillian Lansing's going to be there. She's a friend of Shane and his wife's… and she's single. Jillian's a good looking woman with a heart as big as all of Lexington. She's about your age too."

"You are as bad as my parents. Why are you trying to hook me up with a female?" Simba demanded, narrowing his eyes.

"Not sure," Will admitted with a grin. "It just seems the thing to do today. Jillian's like one of mine now. It would make me happy to see her happy."

Simba shook his head. "I don't know, Will. A beautiful, good-hearted woman in her mid-thirties who hasn't married? Something must be wrong with her."

"You were here when Jackson Lansing died in that plane crash out at the airport, weren't you?"

Simba nodded, remembering the tragedy. "Yes. I remember that happening—basketball player and his wife. He had just taken a coaching job here at UK."

"Right," Will said. "Jillian is his sister. Shane's wife is the wife's sister. Jillian and Reesa have been raising Jackson Lansing's kids since it happened. Four kids is a lot to deal with. Doesn't leave much time for dating."

Simba let loose a low whistle. "That's tough on them... and admirable. Family is more important than ever in our jaded world."

"I know. Shane had a difficult time talking Reesa into marrying him. She was named the children's guardian in the will and Jillian provided for them financially. Reesa sold her car and Jillian sold her house to make the situation work."

"The woman sold her house to care for children not her own? She is a goddess for that alone," Simba said with a laugh.

"Jillian deserves to have a good man in her life. You're a good man, Simba. Can you beat that logic?"

"Mr. Larson, you're in the wrong line of work. You should open a dating service."

Will chuckled as he stood. "No, this was just a one-off spontaneous decision. I came looking for a favor today. Maybe I'm just paying it back. Thanks for looking at the rhino."

"Any time—I mean that," Simba said sincerely, as he stood and reached out a hand, grinning when Will shook it again. "I'll come have a look at her. If things work out, I'll invite you to my wedding."

"Good. Dress nice. Jillian's always decked out. Fashion is serious business for that female."

"Thank you for the tip. I will search my closet for appropriate clothes," Simba said dryly with an eye roll. "I'm beginning to think my parents really did send you to torture me."

"They didn't. See you Saturday, Simba," Will said and walked out laughing.

"Send me a picture when the feet are fixed. I'd like to see what the artist does with them."

"You bet," Will promised as he headed out the door.

6

JILLIAN WALKED THROUGH THE HOUSE, GRATEFUL THAT SHE NO longer lived with her parents. She'd sold her house when her brother had died and used the money to help her nieces and nephews. Reesa and Shane had married and gotten legal custody of the kids. Shane's amazing income had lessened the burden on both her and Reesa. Now she was renting a condo while she saved to buy again.

Her parents had tried to talk her into staying with them—well, her mother had anyway. But her mother tended to hover and offer unsolicited advice on every decision of her life.

Today though, no one seemed to be in the house. Granted, she was a bit early for dinner. Rather than staying late, she'd left work on time for once to get her nails done. "Mama? Are you home?"

When there was no answer from the sitting room or the formal living room next to it, Jillian wandered through the hallway to the kitchen. The oven was on and cooking something that smelled wonderful. She moved into the dining room where she stopped short and stared at the four elegant place settings meticulously set on the impressively decorated table instead of the normal three casual ones. That could only mean one thing.

Jillian groaned at the implications of the additional china. It made her instantly regret agreeing to come to dinner. She'd been in meetings all week and gotten almost no real work done. She'd packed it all up this afternoon and brought it home with her to catch up on it over the weekend.

Jillian stared at the table and chewed her full bottom lip. Talking to a stranger sounded like too much work tonight even if she did get to eat whatever was in the oven that smelled so good. What if it was their new minister again—the widowed man in his mid-fifties that her mom thought was such great marriage material? The idea of seeing him held zero appeal.

She scratched her head and then shook it. "I can't do this—not tonight—not even for great food."

Jillian turned around and made her way back to the sitting room where she'd left her purse and keys when she came in. She gathered them up and headed back to her car.

Sheer relief chased the guilt away after she'd sent a text message to her mother saying she had to work. It was only a tiny social lie—more like an omission. She did have to work just not tonight.

Tonight she was too restless to focus on mundane tasks. She'd work tomorrow before heading to the gallery opening. Tonight she was going to go find food that smelled as good as her mother's and some male company of her own damn choosing.

"Now that's a Friday night agenda I can live with," Jillian said as she backed out of the driveway.

When the doorbell woke him, Joe decided the person ringing it needed to die. Still feeling hung over from too much work and not enough rest, Joe roused himself from the couch and stumbled to the door.

"Who the hell's there?" Joe demanded tersely.

"I brought your dinner," came an equally terse reply.

Joe grumbled loudly as he undid all the locks. "Why does the fucking pizza place around the block always get the apartment numbers wrong? I swear I'm buying a house next week and getting out of this place."

His weary eyes widened at the woman standing at his threshold with a bag in her hands. His nose twitched as his belly growled over the food's smell.

But he was vulnerable—too vulnerable—to deal with her tonight. "Sorry, Lady. You got the wrong house. I didn't order takeout," he said, firming his mouth.

"What in the world have you been doing? You look like hell," Jillian said flatly, eyeing him up and down.

Joe scrubbed a hand over his face. "Too much work this week and not enough sleep."

Jillian nodded. "Good thing I brought food then. We're not eating it in the hall though. Let me in, Joseph."

"Maybe you should look for better company tonight, Jillian. I'm not feeling very friendly."

Jillian rolled her eyes and used her full figure to push him out of her way. "You're hungry and obviously exhausted. You'll rest better after you eat."

"I didn't say you could come in," Joe stated sourly, closing the door to keep his neighbors from hearing more of their conversation.

"Yeah, I noticed. Lucky for you, I'm choosing to overlook your rude ass behavior," she replied as she walked into Joe's messy kitchen and shoved a stack of dirty dishes aside on the counter. She set down the bag full of Chinese food she'd stopped and bought on her way over. "I'll make us some plates once I find some clean ones. You need to hire some help when you work this hard. This mess is emotionally disturbing. I don't know how you can handle it."

"Jillian..." Joe began, but hushed when she turned a determined chocolate gaze in his direction. His mouth twitched when she lifted a finger with a long, red-painted nail and pointed to the couch. What was he? Her dog?

"Sit down and quit complaining. I'm not leaving yet. You might as well quit fighting with me on this because you will never out-stubborn me. I bought enough food for an army so sit down and hush while I get it ready for us."

Giving up, Joe went to his couch and flopped down onto it again. He'd finished the renovations at Will's mid-afternoon which had been some solid work, but that wasn't what had worn him down. He'd also been working on the wooden rhino's tiny feet well into the wee hours for a couple nights. Sleep simply hadn't gotten to happen much. He pushed through his fatigue to finish at Will's only because he needed to be doing an actual paying job.

"Why are you here, Jillian? It's freaking Friday night. Don't you have a chocolate-covered date waiting anxiously for you somewhere?" Joe demanded.

Jillian stopped spooning out food and looked over at him to glare. "You're just spoiling for a big old fight, aren't you? Now I could give you one—never doubt that—but I really just wanted friendly male company while I ate dinner. I didn't come here to debate my dating preferences again."

Chastised over his meanness, Joe leaned back and closed his eyes. "You shouldn't be here at all and yet you keep showing up. I don't even know why you *are* here. I don't fit your five year plan, remember?"

"You're surly and sarcastic. I don't know why I keep coming back either," Jillian said, scrounging in the refrigerator. "Plus… all you ever have in this house is beer. Not a lot of women drink beer, Joseph. Buy a couple bottles of wine. It doesn't cost that much more than beer."

"If you're looking for girly booze, there's a bottle of vodka in the freezer and some soda in the pantry," Joe said wearily.

"Yay for me. There may be hope for you yet," Jillian said, twisting the top off two tall beers. She carried his heaping plate of food to the coffee table and set it down. She handed Joe one of the beers and put the second beer next to his plate.

Joe frowned as he took the beer from fingers. "You're going to make someone a great wife one day."

Despite his dripping sarcasm, Jillian couldn't deny the little frisson of pleasure his comment generated in her gut. She looked at Joe and shook her head. "No woman deserves to put up with your grumpy ass. Eat your food before it gets cold."

"Have you always been so bossy?"

Back in his miniscule kitchen once more, Jillian threw ice in the biggest clean glass she could find and poured it a third full of chilled vodka before topping it off with lemon-lime soda. Maybe drinking would dampen her urge to kill him. "I've always known when I was right about something. Like I am tonight about you. Now quit complaining and eat. Your *hangry* ass is nearly intolerable."

Joe snorted as she gracefully sashayed to his couch in her short plaid skirt and three inch stilettos. She gracefully sat down next to him and put her plate of food on the table at the same time. The woman moved through life on her own terms. His admiration of her body knocked down the emotional walls he kept building, but it was Jillian's self-confidence and ease that appealed to him most. He was a calmer, happier version of himself when she was near.

"Woman, you are female grace personified. Any man would be happy just watching you walk around his house all day. Even my grumpy ass can appreciate that."

Jillian sighed long and shook her head. No way was she taking that comment seriously. "Eat, Joseph. Just... eat. I had a hard week too. Everything on my desk got covered in coffee today and I snagged this skirt—one of my favorite skirts—on a bathroom stall door."

Joe laughed. "At least you didn't break a nail," he said with fresh snark.

"Actually, I did, which is why I left work early to go get it repaired. All fixed now though. See?"

He laughed when Jillian folded her hand and showed him her middle finger. The shiny red end spoke to the truth of her manicured talons. Joe grinned as she lifted her plate and began to eat. "At least you got your priorities straight," he told her. "An elegant woman like yourself can't be walking around with broken fingernails."

Jillian set down her fork before reaching over and pinching his arm as hard as she could. It was a letdown when Joe laughed instead of yelping. She turned her full attention to her plate. Maybe coming here had been a bad idea. His cynical comments and sarcasm were grating on her nerves... and hurting her feelings. Why did she keep coming here? He was right to keep asking her that question, but she honestly didn't know the answer. Joseph McEldowney stirred up too many emotions in her to see anything clearly.

"If talking shit was your plan to get rid of me, it's working," Jillian warned.

Joe turned away and studied the plate of food on the table. Was that his plan to get rid of her? "Maybe I'm trying not to give you a chance to break my heart."

Jillian's fork fell from her fingers to rattle against her plate.

She looked at the man next to her. "Where in the hell did that idea come from? I'm not going to do that. I just... I had a hard week and I wanted to spend a few hours with someone whose company I like—*normally*. Can't that be reason enough to bring you dinner?"

Joe snorted as he lifted his plate again. She wanted his company? More like she wanted sex with him. He was reluctant to get that involved because Jillian didn't want him to be a permanent part of her life. It was ironic that not so long ago her casual attitude would have seemed like a perfect deal to him. He was obviously losing his edge.

"I've been hanging around Shane too long," Joe mused as he began to eat again.

"Will you stop whining for pity's sake? You and Shane can analyze my motives later," Jillian said in exasperation. "After we eat, I'll scoot. I'm sorry you had a hard week. I'm sorrier that I screwed up your pity party."

Joe sighed when her words scored a direct hit. "I'm sorry you had a hard week too. The food is good. Thank you."

Jillian nodded to let Joe know she heard. To lighten the mood, she used her fork to steal a pork dumpling from his plate. "You haven't even tried these little pockets of heaven. They're amazing." She relaxed when he laughed at her thievery. "Do you even like Chinese food?"

"It's okay. I prefer Mexican," Joe answered, using his fork to snitch one of her coconut shrimp.

"Me too, usually," Jillian said, going back to her own food. "But you got to admit these spicy little chicken bites are very tasty. I'd kung pao and deep fry my entire plate if I could, but steamed and grilled don't pile on the pounds."

"Your pounds are in all the right places. Don't be trying to lose them."

"They're in the right places now, but I'm sure they're

planning to move around in the future. That's going to send me to the gym and I hate going there."

Chuckling for the first time in days, Joe set his fork down on the plate and reached out to turn Jillian's face to his. He searched her eyes and once again saw a mirror of his own confusion in them.

"I'm sorry that I'm a grumpy ass. Thanks for dinner. It's delicious." He leaned over and gently touched his lips to hers. "And so are you," Joe said softly as he pulled away.

His chest hurt when Jillian didn't reply to his sexy praise. Based on their previous encounters, he hadn't expected her too. No matter how romantic or loving he got, Jillian just didn't react. *This* was the reality of their relationship. He'd be an idiot to forget her motivation to keep an emotional distance between them.

To keep from picking that fight Jillian had accused him of wanting, Joe picked up the remote and tuned the TV to a sports channel. Beside him, Jillian went on eating and didn't comment on his choice to end their discussion.

She was sending mixed signals and yet wouldn't keep clear. No male in the world would have blamed him for ignoring her... or for falling asleep again almost as soon as he'd finished eating. Between the food and the two beers, he found himself once more at the mercy of his body's need to rest.

Maybe now Jillian would see how incompatible they were and leave him alone so he could get over her.

7

THE RINGING DOORBELL WOKE HIM FROM SLEEP A SECOND TIME.

Joe rolled toward the sound and promptly fell into the floor, tangled up in some old blanket he didn't recognize. Glancing around reassured him he was still in his own place. He got to his feet and hustled to the half bath off the entry because it was closer than the one in his bedroom. He relieved himself while the doorbell chimed two more times.

Stomping out of the bathroom, he scooped the blanket from the floor and tossed it next to the pillow he'd obviously used since his neck wasn't stiff this morning.

Not even bothering to check the peep-hole or call out, he just yanked it open. "Look, Jillian… *Dad?*"

"Surprise," his father said dryly, brandishing a cardboard carrier with two large coffees in it. "Who's Jillian?"

"A friend I was rude to yesterday," Joe grumbled, stepping aside to let his father in. "I'm going to have to clear you a place. Apparently, I slept on the couch last night. It was one of those weeks."

When the door was closed behind his father, Joe walked to the couch and stacked the bedclothes at one end. "There. Sit."

"I brought coffee. Forgot the creamer though."

"I have milk—I think. Let me check. I was too busy to shop last week."

"Well, it's Saturday. Maybe you can get to it today."

"Maybe," Joe said, non-committal. He stopped in the kitchen and noted that the counters were clear and the dishes were done. There was only one person who could have done them. The question was why had she done them? Had she felt sorry for him?

A quick peek into the dishwasher revealed it was haphazardly loaded but all the dirty dishes were in there. Detergent had been added too but the machine hadn't been run. Ignoring his urge to restack everything more neatly, Joe closed the dishwasher door and pushed the button to start the cycle. It was odd to know someone else had done his chores while he slept. That sure as hell had never happened before.

In the refrigerator, he located milk. The Chinese food leftovers from their meal were stacked neatly on an otherwise barren shelf. There seemed to be enough food for a whole other meal. How much food had Jillian bought?

He remembered nothing outside of eating and arguing with her. He'd turned on the TV, finished his meal, and hadn't said much to Jillian beyond that point.

He started back to the couch with the milk and then something dawned on him. The dead bolt on the door had been thrown when he'd let his father inside. There was only one way that could have happened.

Joe glanced in the direction of his bedroom but didn't dare go investigate with his father here. His heart thumped at the idea that Jillian had stayed and slept in his bed last night. It thumped harder at the possibility he maybe could have shared it with her.

But that was a crazy, wasn't it? Hadn't he already made the decision never to take it that far? Maybe he'd let her out of the apartment and in his tiredness forgotten about doing so.

Still wondering, Joe sat next to his father and handed over the mostly empty carton of milk. "Use the rest. I need it strong and black today," Joe said.

Beside him, his father snickered. Ignoring his father's bad sense of humor, Joe lifted his coffee and took a sip. "What time is it?"

"Seven-thirty. I was trying to catch you before you went out on a job."

Joe nodded. That meant he'd slept for at least fourteen hours counting the nap before Jillian had shown up. He sipped and sighed at the lost time.

He glanced toward the second bedroom that he'd turned into a makeshift workshop. With Jillian wandering around his apartment while he slept, he was doubly glad now that he'd installed that locking door. He wasn't ready for her to know about his carving... or really for anyone to know what he was doing. He hadn't even told Shane.

Not that Shane would have taken in the fact that Joe was starting to make art. His friend knew nothing these days except that soon Reesa was going to have their baby. The tiny woman was about to pop and Shane was on the verge of a new father meltdown. No matter how busy his schedule, Joe made time to talk Shane nearly every day.

"What was so important you needed to see me, Dad? I can't remember the last time you came by the apartment."

"Me neither," his father said with some amazement, setting his coffee down. "But this wasn't something I wanted to tell you over the phone."

Joe sipped his coffee as he studied the man who donated genes to create him. They had the same red hair and freckles across their nose—the same rustic red beards when they grew them. His father's hair and beard were dotted with silver now. The only drastic difference between them was their eyes. Joe had inherited his mother's eyes... and her survivalist nature... which was why he was wishing now that he hadn't answered the damn door.

"My ticker is in trouble, Joe. I'm supposed to have heart surgery next month. If I kick off and don't make it, will you look after Melanie and the kids? I'm leaving them enough to pay normal bills but the insurance is not going to cover college or cars. Melanie's never worked so I don't see her bringing home much bacon even if she did get a job. I figured since you probably aren't going to settle down for a while that you might not mind looking after your other family."

"What do you mean? I'm barely turning thirty. Lots of men don't settle down until well after that," Joe said.

His father lifted a shoulder. "Never saw you with any woman more than a few weeks. Figured you liked your bachelor life. Truth be told—I've always been a bit envious of your casual approach to females."

Joe grunted. With every woman he'd dated, he'd been looking for love, but he wasn't telling his father that. The man would have had a heart attack laughing at him. "I'm not being as casual as it seems. It's called being picky, and last time I checked, it wasn't illegal."

Joe looked at his father—really looked at him. Heart surgery... no wonder the man looked so old at fifty. He felt instant and genuine sympathy for Melanie and the kids, but nearly none for his parent with the problem. Hearing about his father's illness was like listening to a stranger in the doctor's office talking about theirs.

His father saluted him with what was left of his coffee. "It's probably called not wanting to be tied to a ball and chain. Pretty smart way to live if you can manage it. I kept getting attached to the women I dated," his father said.

Joe shook his head. His mother had died of cancer but had lived dead most of her life. Her heart had been broken by his father's departure. She'd never remarried or even dated that he knew. It had been a terrible waste of a wonderful woman.

And for what? His father hadn't been worth that. No man or woman was worth that.

Despite his mother's devotion, Joe still remained grateful that Will Larson had intervened in the spiraling hell of his parent's marriage before something worse had happened. Even as a teenager their dissatisfaction with each other had been obvious to him. Joe had been nothing but relieved when his father had moved out and never returned. There had been a lot less yelling and no angry fists raised in threats after the man had gone.

But it wasn't just bad childhood memories that made Joe apathetic toward his father. The man hadn't bothered to come to his mother's funeral. Only his stepmother had found the courage to come see him and extend condolences. It had softened Joe's heart toward the younger woman and softened it toward the half-siblings that had come along while he was in college. He was kind when he saw them which was as little as he could get by with doing.

But seeing them all as his true family and as people he had a responsibility to? That was never going to happen. Even if he did think of himself as a decent human being, he was not a Larson. They were the only men he knew who could manage that level of forgiveness.

"Melanie can always call me. If anything happens to you, I'll remind her of it," Joe finally said.

"Guess that's all I can ask," his father replied.

Joe nodded. "I'm sure you'll be fine. Doctors are miracle workers these days."

Though he'd already suspected she'd stayed, Joe still stared in shock when Jillian walked out of his bedroom fully dressed and wearing her heels. Her hair was mussed and her makeup was missing, but the woman looked amazing. It was also clear Jillian didn't give a shit what either him or his father thought of her appearance. Her self-confidence was just one of many things he liked about her.

"Good morning," Joe said, awestruck more than ever. Damn, he doubly wished like hell he hadn't answered the door. If his father hadn't been here, he'd have stood and kissed her.

"Good morning," Jillian answered carefully, her wary gaze going to the older replica of the man she liked before it returned to Joe. "You weren't lying about being exhausted. You passed out on the couch after you ate. I'd had too much vodka to drive so I stayed over. What time is it? I brought several hours of work home."

"You've got time. It's still early," Joe said. He held his coffee out to her. A sighing Jillian walked over and gingerly slipped the cup from his fingers to take a bracing sip. "Anything in here?" she asked. "We don't know each other's morning habits, but I drink mine black."

Joe opened his mouth to tell her how much he wanted to know everything about her, but closed it promptly when his father laughed.

"Of course, you take it black. That makes perfect sense," his father said with a grin.

Appalled at his father's crude attempt at humor, Joe turned and glared at the still chuckling man. The meanness of his own actions toward Jillian last night now broadsided his conscience. She'd taken care of him and now woke this morning to this shit.

Epic fail on his part. He should have checked his bedroom and run his irreverent old man off before Jillian had to deal with him.

Joe turned his attention back to Jillian and stood up. She took one more sip of his coffee, lifted her chin, and handed the cup back. "I better get going. My sense of humor isn't feeling so sharp this morning. My mouth might get the better of me."

Joe ran a hand over his head as his face heated with mortification. "Don't rush off just because my father's being an ass. He can leave instead."

"It's true. I am often an ass, but even you have to see what you said was ironic," Joe's father said agreeably. "But I'm sorry if I hurt your feelings, honey."

"*Honey?*" Jillian's mouth twisted. "So you're both racist and sexist, huh? I've wallowed in the mud yelling at people like you all my life, but I'm not doing it this time. No, I am not. I have a lot better things to be doing on a Saturday morning."

After she'd retrieved her purse, Joe put a hand on Jillian's arm as he walked her to the door. He could tell she was in hurry to get away and didn't blame her for it.

"My father really is an ass, but after last night, you probably think I'm not much better," he whispered.

Jillian stumbled on her stilettos as she rounded on him. She didn't bother to lower her voice. Let his father hear her. She couldn't bring herself to care.

"Joseph, that man is nothing but a sperm donor. I have one of those myself. The difference is mine doesn't make black jokes. He makes white ones. A racist is a racist no matter what color he is. When it comes to being sexist, our fathers are probably a close match. You're a moody man and often sarcastic, but you are absolutely not like them. Don't even go there or I really will get pissed at you."

For giving him even that much dispensation, Joe wanted to

pull her close, hug her tightly, and never let go. Instead, he lifted Jillian's fingers to his mouth and kissed them. "I'm sorry you woke up to this. I don't know what else to say. He dropped by… and I…"

Jillian put a hand on his chest. "I know you had to let him in because that's what good children do, but don't apologize to me for his bad behavior. My father verbally tortured my sister-in-law until Jackson quit bringing his family around. When my brother died, he hadn't talked to our father in months. Everyone makes their own choices, Joseph. That man who looks a little bit like you has made his."

Joe nodded as she slipped out to escape, but it felt like Jillian was slipping away from him altogether. What woman would want to stay and deal with shit his father dished out?

He waited until Jillian disappeared before closing the door and counting to ten.

"Nice going with that one, Joe. Woman has great legs. Bet she's feisty as hell in bed too," his father said, chuckling again. "Why in fuck's sake were you sleeping on the couch?"

Jillian was right. Enough was enough—especially on a Saturday morning. He had better things to do too. Joe opened the door again and pointed outside. "It's time for you to leave," he told his father.

His father smirked as he stood. "I blame this social guilt shit on your wimpy mother. She never let you develop a real sense of humor."

Joe pulled himself straight and curled his fingers into his palm. "*Never* talk badly about my mother again or I will beat you. And Jillian is a good friend that you insulted with your crassness. The only reason I'm not decking you right now is because of your health issues. Send me a text when you're having surgery. Tell Melanie to call me when it's over. Other than that, don't come around again without calling me first. I don't want you in my life. That hasn't changed."

Joe felt nothing but relief when his snickering father walked by him to leave as requested. He slammed the door behind his old man, but the minor show of anger wasn't going to fix what had just happened.

Now Jillian knew exactly what kind of family he came from. If anything could have stopped her from seeing him as a man she might love, meeting the racist and sexist bottom-dweller swimming in his gene pool likely had done it.

8

THERE WAS A SEA OF PEOPLE MILLING ABOUT THE GALLERY BUT Joe's gaze went to Jillian like he'd tracked her there. She was wearing a full-skirted black and white dress that hit her legs mid-calf. On her feet were multi-jeweled tone flats instead of her typical tall heels. The outfit made her look a little more vulnerable than usual. He wondered how much shorter it would make her standing next to him. Would he be looking down into her eyes?

He was heading toward her to find out when a large hand jerked him to a fault.

"Have you seen Reesa?" Shane demanded.

"No, I just got here," Joe said with a laugh, peeling Shane's massive fingers off his bicep. Even through his jacket, Shane's large grip was fierce.

Like a prairie dog popping upright, Shane raised up as tall as possible as he looked over the heads of the gallery patrons. Joe laughed at the action. "You're not going to find her that way, bro. You need to be crawling on the floor to look for her."

"She's not that short," Shane denied, turning to glare down at his friend.

Joe rubbed his mouth to banish the grin that threatened. "Of course not. My bad. Five feet is like Amazon size on a woman." Joe snapped his fingers. "Hey—maybe Reesa's hiding from you. The woman can't stand it when you hover. Have you checked the women's bathroom?"

Shane frowned and turned to glare at his best friend. "Do you not understand that the baby could come anytime? I don't want her delivering before the C-section date. We're less than a month away and you know how she is. She won't take it easy unless I make her."

"You're a hot mess of worry, aren't you?" Joe asked.

"I prefer to think of it as vigilance."

Laughing at Shane's defensiveness, Joe lifted a finger and pointed to where Reesa was now waddling up to stand in front of Jillian. The couple next to her seemed to know them both. Reesa smiled politely, nodded, and answered questions while Jillian watched all the participants with sharp wolf eyes. "You can relax. Jillian's on-guard."

Shane turned in the direction of Joe's pointing and narrowed his gaze. "You're right. She is on-guard. Those are Jillian's parents. They don't like Reesa."

"Oh," Joe said, his stomach dropping. Jillian's parents were here?

It seemed Jillian was having a shitty day all around. He certainly didn't need to make it worse by getting in front of her bigoted parents—not after she'd had to deal with his bigoted father today.

Joe forced a smile to his lips as he slapped Shane on the back. "Better go rescue Reesa and Jillian. Remind her parents that Reesa married one of her own kind."

Shane glared. "Not funny, Joe."

"No, it's not. Jillian told me that's what they're like. There are no secrets here, Larson—just closet racists of all kinds."

"Maybe, but I can tell you that Jillian's parents don't hate me because I'm white," Shane said firmly. "They hate me because I made enough money to help Reesa keep full custody of all the kids. Trust me—they would have hated me for that no matter what color I was. My income screwed up their plans to get custody of Zach and Chelsea. Her father badly wanted to control Zach's basketball career at UK."

Joe grunted at the irony as he shook his head. "Do you realize how lucky you are? Will and Ellen were great parents to you, and they married well the second time too. Luke helped you in court. Jessica loves both you and Michael. I'm just glad I got to see how real love is supposed to work. I can only imagine how messed up I'd be if you and your mostly normal family hadn't been part of my life."

"Normal is debatable," Shane said with a chuckle. He clapped a hand on Joe's shoulder. "And you're still part of our life. Look—Jillian's parents are walking away. Thank God."

Joe grinned. "I think I'm going to get Jillian a glass a wine to help her bear it when you end up making your wife mad at you again."

"What are talking about? Reesa loves me," Shane said with confidence.

"I know, but that doesn't mean she won't get mad at you hovering over her. I've seen that too many times not to know exactly how things are going to go down if you start fussing," Joe reminded him.

Shrugging off the warning, Shane walked swiftly toward the women. Joe laughed and headed to the caterers who were pouring drinks. He ordered one white and one red before carrying both toward where he'd seen Jillian standing.

Reesa and Shane were no doubt off arguing by now. He

stopped a few feet away and hid in the crowd when he noticed Will and another guy step forward and start talking to her. Jillian was shaking hands and smiling at the new guy who Joe heard professing to be a UK art professor. His accent wasn't totally American but that probably only added to the good-looking academic's appeal to women.

Not liking the jealousy he was feeling, Joe took a sip of one glass and then a sip of the other. The wine didn't change anything... or banish his possessive feelings. The mocha-skinned academic looked damn good next to her. The guy was dressed nearly as well as Jillian was tonight, had a charming smile, and best of all, he fit the standard guy she usually dated right down to his polished shoes.

Add in the nice laugh and the way he was looking at Jillian and everything about him added up to the UK professor being the kind of ideal man the woman he now loved had been looking for. The academic would fit in with her parents too. No fights over interracial mixing. No racism to overcome. Jillian wouldn't have to defend her choice of him. Tough shit for him, but Joe prided himself on being a hardcore realist.

Sighing, Joe watched as Will walked off. He wasn't surprised the guy remained behind to keep chatting. Will had been matchmaking. It was pretty obvious to anyone who knew Jillian was still single and dating. Joe might as well get his part of the awkwardness over.

Ignoring the academic, Joe walked to Jillian and held out both glasses. "I didn't know if you liked red or white wine, but at least I brought you wine instead of beer."

"Hello, Joseph. You didn't tell me you were coming tonight," Jillian said sharply, slipping the glass of red from his fingers.

"I forgot to mention it when I saw you," Joe said casually.

Still smiling, he turned to the man and put out a hand. "Hi. I'm Joseph McEldowney—a friend of Jillian's."

"Simba James. Nice to meet you," Simba said, shaking his hand.

"I confess I heard you saying you were an art professor at UK when I walked up. Any of your work in here?" Joe asked.

"My work? No," Simba said with surprise, shaking his head. "My paintings are not of this caliber yet. In recent years, I have spent too much time teaching and not enough time making art."

"I bet you're a great teacher. Your voice is easy on the ears. Great suit too, by the way."

"Thank you. Perhaps I should get some wine as well," Simba said.

"Sure," Joe said with a grin, lifting his glass in the direction of the caterers. "Bar is just a few steps that way. I'll keep Jillian company until you get back. No worries."

Joe's mouth twitched when Simba smiled uncomfortably and nodded before he moved off.

Jillian sipped her wine and glared at Joseph over her glass. "What was that all about? Simba probably thinks you were hitting on him."

"Well, why wouldn't I? Simba's handsome and seems like a nice guy," Joe said with a laugh.

"Yes. He does," Jillian agreed.

"Snappy dresser too. He looks good next to you, Jillian."

Jillian lifted her chin. "And what's that supposed to mean?"

Joe looked around the room until his gaze rested on her parents. "It means that Professor James is a guy you wouldn't have to defend to your parents. He's perfect for your plan. Right?"

"My plan is *my* plan," Jillian nearly hissed. "My plan is none of your business. And you know nothing about my plan."

"We've trolled the same bars. I've watched you date for years," Joe said, turning to meet her gaze. "And that's why I came over here. I wanted to tell you to go after the academic if he appeals to you. We both knew from the beginning that our attraction wasn't going anywhere. It's time we moved on and stopped tormenting each other with our half-ass, incredibly dumb obsession with each other."

Jillian snorted as she sipped her wine. "Your lecture sounds like a break-up speech, but according to you, we never had a thing anyway. I'm confused, Joseph."

Joe looked away as he nodded. "Yeah. I was confused for a while too, but I'm not anymore. My father stopping by this morning helped me remember how complicated real life is. I don't like my father as a person but he's part of my life. Just like your parents are a part of yours. Those bigoted realities aren't going to change for us. Fighting with our parents for something as casual as we have going on between us doesn't seem very smart."

Joe stepped closer when he saw Simba headed back their way. He didn't have much time. "You were a fantasy woman to me—someone I wanted badly, but deep down also knew I couldn't really have—not for the long haul. Life doesn't always have to be this hard, Jillian. You gave me a chance and my racist father was your reward. Give the freaking academic a chance. You deserve for life to be the way you want it to be and for it to be a little damn easier."

"And you'd be alright if I dated him?" Jillian asked softly.

"Yeah, I'll be alright," Joe answered quietly. "And so will you."

He turned and toasted Simba's return. "Hello again, Simba James. Now that you're back, I'm going to go mingle." Joe turned and boldly kissed Jillian on the cheek. He could tell the action had shocked her. "Think about cutting yourself a break, honey. You deserve one."

Jillian stared at him without answering. Not able to handle the situation any longer, Joe turned and left before he changed his mind.

~

"JOSEPH IS A FRIEND?" SIMBA ASKED, WHEN THE CRAZY MAN HAD walked away.

"Yes," Jillian replied, forcing her gaze back to the man talking to her. "And before you ask—no, he's not gay. He was just messing with you."

Simba chuckled. "Because he wanted to talk to you alone," he concluded.

Jillian nodded. "Are all professors as perceptive as you?"

Simba shrugged. "I well know what it is like to want to talk to a beautiful woman alone. I am grateful for his timely departure and thoughtfulness."

Jillian rolled her eyes internally. The guy was nice times ten. And yes, he was definitely handsome. If Joseph hadn't shown up tonight, she'd have happily spent the evening charming the professor. Instead, she now wanted to track down the red-haired idiot and yell at him for presuming to tell her how to live her life. Only she couldn't with her parents watching her every move. Well, she could, but...

Sighing at her unwillingness to stir up things, Jillian shook her head. "I hate to tell you this, Simba, but our talking alone thing is going to last about twenty more seconds. My parents are headed this way. I'll just apologize in advance for their nosy questions and their assumptions that we're secretly planning to elope."

Simba laughed. "I take it they are pushing you to marry."

"Only because they want grandchildren before I get too old to have them. They don't care about my happiness. Don't even begin to think that."

Simba laughed louder. "I think we have much in common, Jillian."

Jillian sighed. She was not going to lead this nice man on. "We might, but…"

"Jillian, you're still standing in the same spot we left you. You're supposed to wander around at these things," her mother said as she fussed. "Who's your friend?"

After introductions, she and Simba didn't get to speak another word to each other. Her father asked a thousand questions about his job. Her mother invited him to dinner and kept insisting he come. Professor Simba James was so polite, handsome, and interesting that being subtle probably never crossed their mind.

But it was not surprising that her growing interest in Joseph had gone completely unnoticed by their radar. One look is all it had taken for them to conclude Simba was a good prospect for their unmarried daughter. Even seeing Joseph kissing her cheek wouldn't have caused a blip in their minds. Joseph was not someone her parents would have ever considered worthy as a date. Yet to her, he was fast becoming the only man she wanted to spend time with.

Jillian studied Simba as he fielded questions. He was polite, firm, and handled her parents being nosy with a level of calm poise she'd rarely witnessed in a man. Her quiet sigh over her disinterest in his niceness fortunately wasn't audible over her mother's gushing at every word Simba spoke.

What was wrong with her? Joseph was right. She should give Simba a chance.

God only knew the charming professor would improve her dating life. If Simba didn't ask her to do his laundry or force her to eat at sushi restaurants, he would be way better than the last couple of men she'd spent any time with.

But would Simba ever appeal to her the way Joseph innately did? Would she think of Simba so often during the day that she'd go invade his home uninvited just to see him? Would she put up with his irritating man shit simply because his eyes followed her when she walked and his lips told her she was beautiful?

A woman could get used to that kind of attention—the kind that made her feel as beautiful as she kept hearing she was. Why didn't more men understand that?

Dating Simba would be a good decision. There was no doubt about it and she could tell he was interested in her. The charming, well-spoken professor dressed impeccably and was handsome. More than all that though, he checked off nearly all the boxes on the list she'd been compiling since she'd been old enough to date.

Her heart though... her heart was wondering where Joseph had disappeared to after he'd recited his break-up speech. And it was also wondering if Reesa had been right about her leaving some very important things off her list. Things like humor. Things like being passionate enough to fight and fair enough to apologize. Things like... well, like love.

Not that she loved Joseph. No. She didn't even know him that well. She'd made sure of that, hadn't she? She didn't know his favorite color or what kind of music he listened to. And despite all their fooling around—and the man was a master at that—she hadn't found out which side of the bed he slept on. Well, that wasn't completely true. But she hadn't found out the fun way.

The man hadn't been lying about being exhausted. Because of her giant vodka drink, she'd had to crash in his bedroom and his bed, especially since Joseph had passed out on the couch without so much as saying goodnight.

His one pathetic nightstand beside the queen-sized bed had provided a big clue if not the answer to which side he favored. She noted his closet had needed organizing too because the door to it was left wide open. How was she not supposed to look? It would take her under an hour to fix his closet if he'd just install some proper shelving in there.

Jillian had to admit that his pristine bathroom had been a very pleasant surprise. That was unexpected, especially since the man had let doing his dishes slide for what had looked like at least a week. She'd barely gotten them all into the dishwasher. What in the world had kept him so busy? Did that happen all the time?

Jillian rubbed the center of her chest and did her best to bring her attention to the man in front of her. It was smarter than dwelling on the man she really shouldn't be thinking about as much as she was.

9

THREE WEEKS LATER...

"HEY, SHANE." JOE HELD HIS APARTMENT DOOR OPEN AS THE large, angry man stomped inside. After starting his work at UK, Shane wore suits and dress clothes most of the time. Today though Shane was wearing his eyebrow piercings, holey jeans, and a t-shirt that belonged in a rag bag. That material had seen better days back when they were in college.

Shane's scraggly appearance reminded Joe of old times. Yet it also meant Shane wanted to intimidate every person he saw which today included him. His friend was pissed at being pulled away from his pregnant wife against his will. But he'd get over it. The man got angry but it never lasted long.

Joe looked off to keep from laughing when Shane sent his best angry glare in his direction. He heard Shane draw in a frustrated breath and his grin bloomed.

"Okay, I'm here. What was so damn important that I had to come over to your apartment on a Saturday morning? The baby's due date is next week. Chelsea and Brian swore they weren't going anywhere today, but you know how teenagers are. One phone call from a frantic friend and any promise they made me is history."

Struggling to keep his growing amusement out of sight, Joe nodded as gravely as he could and threw the deadbolt to lock them inside. A properly motivated Shane could easily tear the hollow core door off its hinges, but Joe had his way of calming the savage beast inside his best friend.

Joe pointed a finger. "Bro... I hate to break it to you, but you're stuck with me for a few hours. Your wife called me yesterday and begged me to keep you occupied today so she could have some peace. While I'm not one of your graphic novel heroes by any stretch of anyone's imagination, I couldn't refuse her request. That means you're going to have to deal with being here because I can't let you go home until at least mid-afternoon."

Shane sighed and ran a hand through his hair that was a couple months behind in being trimmed. "Reesa called you? You're shitting me."

"No, I'm not, but it's all good. I wanted to see you anyway. That's why I actually agreed to her request rather than try and convince your wife for the hundredth millionth time that your hovering only means you're madly in love with her and care. I'm honoring the bro code as best as I can, but your wife seemed desperate. Reesa made me promise to keep you here for as long as I could. So set your ass down and make the best of it."

"Up yours, McEldowney. I can't believe Reesa called you," Shane groused, flopping down on Joe's dilapidated couch.

"Well, she did," Joe said with conviction, barely keeping his twitching mouth from moving into a wide, told-you-so smile.

Shane grunted in disbelief as he looked around Joe's

apartment. "This place is just as much a wreck as it was when you moved in here. Aren't you ever going to buy some decent chairs? This couch is worn out."

Joe looked around at the shabbiness and shrugged. It wasn't like he entertained masses of people on a regular basis. The rent was cheap and he was saving money by being there.

"Don't worry, Mr. Domesticated. I'll get around to buying new stuff eventually. Instead of buying new chairs for your allegedly picky ass, my savings are currently funding some time off for me while I've been working on a project that isn't paying jack shit. You should be grateful that I bought a bunch of beer after Reesa called me yesterday and confirmed you were coming by."

Shane chose to ignore the fact that his wife conspired with Joe. Pregnancy had made her do a bunch of strange things. He had learned to take them in stride—at least most of them. Conspiring with Joe didn't even make the top ten crazy list.

"Are you doing pro bono work again? You do too much of that, Joe. You have a right to make real money. Do you need another self-worth pep talk?"

Joe laughed at the pro bono question and at the threat of counseling. "I'll pass on the lecture—thanks. And I guess you could call what I'm doing pro bono work. The project I've been working on is personal."

"Are you building a house for yourself? Good. It's about damn time."

"No, Shane. I'm not building a house. If I wanted a house, I'd buy the best one I could afford, and then renovate what I didn't like. I'm not ready to buy a house yet. Guess again."

"Fine. If you're going to keep being mysterious, can I at least get a couple of those beers you bought to lure me over here," Shane said.

"Beer at 10:00 am in the morning?" Joe asked with a laugh.

"Yes. Apparently, I'm not driving for a while, so it doesn't matter if I drink and have to Uber my way to the hospital."

Joe burst out chuckling. "Quit your whining, Larson. Your woman's not leaving the house. Reesa just wanted some alone time. Plus, she said Jillian was coming over, though I'm surprised Jillian's active social life allows for weekend visitations."

Shane sighed and shook his head. He headed to Joe's kitchen and got his own beer from the fridge. "You don't have to posture. Go ahead and ask me about her, you big dork."

"Ask what about who?" Joe tilted his head. "You mean Jillian? I don't have to ask. I know the man she's dating now. I met him at the gallery show last month. He's a UK art professor. The man was ogling her with interest. Hell, he all but asked her out in front of me."

"You're talking about Simba James," Shane said as he opened his beer. "I thought you were talking about the fifty-ish guy her mother keeps pushing off on her."

"What fifty year old guy?" Joe asked with a glare, walking closer. "That's too old for Jillian. She's barely your brother's age."

Shrugging Shane took another drink of his beer. "Jillian hasn't brought the fifty-ish guy around, so I don't know much, but I think he's the minister of their church. I heard he was a widower and that Jillian helped him decorate his house."

Joe frowned. "What the hell happened between Jillian and Simba? He seemed perfect for her and exactly her type. And he was her age. Or, so I thought."

Shane drank half a beer before shrugging again. "I don't think what they had was serious. I'm sure Reesa would have said if it was. She's worried about Jillian though—said that Jillian was acting weird. Of course, Reesa's judgment could be coming from an excess of baby hormones. She's been really strange lately. I'll ask her about Jillian again after the baby gets here."

Joe scrubbed his face. "God, now I see why she was begging me to get you out of her hair. Poor woman. She deserves better."

Shane nodded. "Jillian? Yeah, I don't think any of the guys she's ever dated have made her happy. I don't know why you haven't asked her out. You two have always seemed to have some real chemistry. I used to think you had a big crush on her."

"Damn it, Shane. I wasn't talking about Jillian—I was talking about Reesa. It's bad enough she's carrying another annoying Larson male inside her, but dealing with your asshat comments about baby hormones probably makes her want to kill you. The only thing wrong with her at the moment is that she's too nice to use a club on that hard Larson head of yours."

Shane's beer lowered from his lips as shock overtook him. "A boy? We're having a boy? How the hell do you know that, Joe? Only Jillian knows the sex. We were waiting to know until it was born."

"Fuck me," Joe said bitterly, huffing in disgust over what he'd said. "Jillian told me months ago because she was excited about the baby. I wasn't supposed to tell you or Reesa. Sorry about that. The truth just slipped out when I was chastising you."

"A boy," Shane repeated, his face breaking into a smile. "I'm having a son, Joe. I'm having a son. That's amazing."

Joe grunted in resignation. "Yes. Another hard-headed Larson male is joining the world. Just what we all needed."

Shane laughed at Joe's comment and drank the rest of his beer. He put the glass bottle in the recycle bin and got another from the refrigerator. "Don't worry. I'll pretend surprise when he's born. Reesa will never know I knew before she did."

Joe glared. "Oh, like hell you will. You'll tell her that I told you the minute you get home today. Then you'll laugh your ass off while you watch Jillian kill me for not keeping her secret."

A grinning Shane walked by him as he went back to the couch and set the second beer on the coffee table. "So... now that you've told me your best secret, what else was it you wanted to talk to me about? Any other confessions to make?"

Shaking his head with resignation because he knew he was in big trouble for his slip, Joe walked to his dining room table and picked up the rhino. "Heads up, smartass," he called as he tossed the wooden animal to Shane."

Shane caught it and stared down at it in wonder. "Nice piece. I love all the detail. Did you see how carefully someone carved the feet? That level of detail is the hallmark of a true artist. Where did you buy this?"

Joe snorted. At least Shane wasn't faking his surprise over the rhino. Will had kept his artistic secret. Shane would never be able to fake his surprise at his son's birth. The man didn't have much lying in him. Now brutal honesty—Shane Larson had that in spades.

"For your information, I didn't buy it. I carved it."

Shane looked down at what he held in his hands. "Are you serious? This is amazing."

Joe shrugged. "Your father critiqued it... and made me carve the feet. In my first run at making the rhino, I left the feet plain. Will wasn't having it. I can't say no to him either. He and Reesa should form a damn club."

Grinning, Shane looked at the rhino and then at Joe. "Has anyone else seen this?"

Joe shook his head. "No. Of course not. Who would I show?"

"I don't know. How about the entire world?" Shane asked.

"Shut up," Joe ordered, walking to plop down on the couch

next to Shane. "I'm tired of your smartass remarks." He took the rhino from his friend's fingers. "This is the first piece I ever finished."

"So what have you done in the last three weeks? Is this the personal project you've been working on?" Shane asked carefully as understanding dawned. Obsession with making art at first felt like nothing more than a guilty pleasure. His friend was new to that sensation. Shane was used to getting lost in the magic of pen and ink, and in making the next version of the *Winged Protector*. Next to his family, creating graphic novels was his greatest joy.

"I can show you some other pieces," Joe said quietly, "but you can't tell anyone about what you're seeing. And you can't look at what I'm not ready to share."

"Of course," Shane said sincerely as he nodded in agreement.

Joe got up and fetched a key from a dish on his kitchen counter. He walked to the second bedroom and unlocked it as Shane snickered in surprise.

"You're not allowed to laugh at my work," Joe ordered.

"If it's anything like this rhino, I'm sure it'll be equally amazing. What I'm laughing about is your locked door? Who in the fuck are you hiding your art from? The pizza delivery guy who gets the wrong apartment every time?"

"A man's got a right to lock his damn bedroom door if he wants," Joe replied with a glare, pushing the door open.

Shane got up and walked to the door. "Wow. I can smell the wood. That's such a wonderful smell."

When he walked in, his mouth fell open. Tables and shelves surrounded the room. Carvings in various types of wood were absolutely everywhere. One table was stacked tall and covered with several sheets and two blankets. He'd bet Joe had stashed his in progress work under there and out of sight.

"Holy shit, Joe," Shane said, looking around.

Joe sighed and nodded. "I say that too. I say it every damn time I open the door and see all this. I still can't believe it came from me. I can't seem to stop making them. I've postponed other work for weeks now. This is all I want to do."

Shane walked to a table full of statues. They were each about twelve inches tall. The details were amazing. Women. Men. Groups of people laughing or singing or dancing.

"Joe—I don't know what to say. These are…" Shane turned to look at his friend. Had all this always been inside Joe? A man he'd known since they were six? It was mind-boggling. "These pieces are some of the best African art I've ever seen. Why…"

Joe held up a hand. "Don't bother asking that question because I can't answer it."

Shane turned back and stared at all the statutes. He knew why Joe's mind had made such an artistic choice. Why didn't Joe? Reesa was going to have every instinct she had confirmed when she saw this. And Jillian… Jillian was going to be dumbstruck or impressed or have a meltdown. Anything was possible. "What are you planning to do with all of these?"

Joe lifted both shoulders. "Don't know. My first thought was to pack everything up in a box and shove it in my closet. At the rate I'm making this stuff though, I'm going to have to find space in my storage locker for it. I'm working on some bigger pieces that I know I won't have room to store here unless I spread them around my apartment like decorations. Every option gives me the willies. That's why they're still behind a locked door."

"Joe, I think you're going to find that you can't hide your art forever," Shane said sternly. "Now I'm not telling you what to do exactly, but you have some hellacious talent. Surely, you can see that."

"God, you sound like Will."

Shane snorted. "Thanks. I consider that high praise. Don't change the subject."

"Fine. Don't you mean I've got hellacious audacity?" Joe asked as he shoved both hands in his jeans pockets.

"I hope so. Audacity is helpful to an artist. It takes a big ego to put your work out into the world."

"No. Think about this, Shane. What right does the whitest of white men have to be making what everyone keeps calling African art? I'm the son of an openly racist, sexist man—one of the worst you'll ever meet. I'm hell and far from being African, much less black. Creating the tribal people? That was just therapy for an obsession I can't seem to shake any other way."

Shane shook his head all through Joe's tirade. "Art is whatever that word means to the artist. What right does any artist have to reflect the visions in his mind? Inspiration doesn't care about skin color or ethnicity or anything else really. I mean, look at what you've done here. These are amazing. You're obviously making what's in you to make. Fuck what other people think. Their presumptions are not your problem."

Joe snorted at the irony. "They're especially not my problem if no one ever finds out that I made this stuff. I'm keeping it behind closed doors, Shane. Does that sound like someone who's proud of their work?"

Shane shook his head in denial. "Look, I know this is easy for someone else like me to say and much harder for you to actually live with. Jessica's vagina art is a perfect example. Some think it's beautiful and brave. Others see it as pornographic and obscene. The world is lucky Jessica didn't let anyone's opinion stop her from creating it or sharing it. The message she put out into the world was very healing for women who'd suffered what she did."

"I get that," Joe said quietly. "But it's not just about what you call 'the world', Shane. It's about the shit I'd stir up closer to home if I did anything with this stuff. Can you imagine what my father would say to me and others if he saw what I'd carved? And how would artists of color react to knowing someone as white as me created this?"

Shane moved away from the people statures and to a table full of animals. All kinds of animals. He picked up an Alaskan Malamute with blue eyes. "This dog is not African." He set the dog down and picked up a polished cherry Cardinal with wings stretched out in flight. "This bird is every bit as amazing as the rhino and it's not African either. If you not comfortable with the African pieces, show the rest to the world. It's a shame to waste this."

"I can't, Shane. I just can't. I'm not a real artist."

Shane set down the Cardinal. "Okay. I won't pressure you any further."

"Okay?" Joe asked in stunned shock. "Really?"

Grinning, Shane's head dipped down as he nodded. "Yes. Sharing your art is something only you can decide."

"You won't tell anyone about it though, will you?"

"No. I won't," Shane promised, "but you should. I think you need to talk to other people. At least take your art somewhere and get a professional opinion of it. I'm betting that hearing it from a stranger will change your mind."

Joe looked around the room and shrugged. "I don't know. I'll have to think about it."

"With a talent like you seem to have, I'm sure your Muse isn't going to give you much choice eventually. The world can wait a bit longer for you to come to terms with your destiny," Shane said with a chuckle.

Joe shook his head but at the same time wondered if that were true. So far he hadn't been able to put a single piece away. Not even the rhino.

His mind drifted until he felt Shane turn him and push him

out of the bedroom. "We need beer," he heard Shane say while laughing. After they left the room, Joe stared blankly around. The idea of other people seeing his art scared him far more than he ever would have imagined it would.

He watched Shane lock the bedroom door back and carry the key back to its home on the kitchen counter. The next thing he knew Shane was pressing an open beer into his hands.

"Come sit down before you fall down. I can see you're in shock over my suggestions."

"I'm not brave like you, Shane."

"No, you're braver, Joe. You've had way more to overcome than I have. Despite their divorce, my parents always had my back. Dad and Michael always supported my art. The only stability you've ever had is me."

"Oh, come on," Joe exclaimed. "It's not like I've been suffering. Your family has always made me feel like I belonged."

"Because you do," Shane said with a grin. "But despite you being an honorary Lawson male, I'm not going to nag you to do what you're not ready to do. Just don't let Michael see your work because he's not as patient as Dad and I are. He'd make you take it public."

Joe ran a hand over his hair. "Damn… I never even thought of telling Michael. It's bad enough you and your dad both know. Do you think Will is going to pressure me to share my work?"

Shane shrugged. "Hard to say. You said you'd think about it so I'm going to let that be enough for now. Let's find a game on TV and forget about things for a while. You try and forget your art obsession and I'll try to forget about my wife and unborn son for a couple hours. Since I'm stuck here, we might as well make the most of it and order Chinese food for lunch."

"Chinese?" Joe hadn't eaten Chinese since Jillian had come

by. He'd tossed out the leftovers because they reminded him too much of her. "How about Mexican instead?"

"Sure," Shane said absently, already using the remote to switch channels.

Joe sat on the couch and stared at the TV without seeing a damn thing. All he saw was the unfinished piece hidden under a sheet in the locked room behind them, but when he went to work on it, he never got very far. That had been his problem for three weeks now. The other pieces were just something to fill the time while he thought about how to finish the bigger one.

"NO, MAMA. YOU TALKED ME INTO DECORATING HIS HOUSE. THAT was awkward enough. I'm not going to volunteer to clean it every week too. The man's a widower. That doesn't mean he's helpless."

Jillian frowned as her mother stirred the pot on the stove. Was she really so desperate for food and company that she needed to put up with this same debate twice a week?

"Evelyn, have you seen my green golf shirt?"

"Yes. You donated it to charity last month," her mother said to her father.

Her father frowned at her mother's back. "Why would I do that? That shirt was new. You're making that up to confuse me."

Jillian watched her mother turn from the stove. "Franklin, you said the green was too close to the color of the grass on the golf course. You said you wished you hadn't bought that shirt. I was being a good wife in getting rid of it for you."

"That shirt cost me eighty dollars, Evelyn. You can't be throwing good things away all the time, especially *my* things."

"Which is why I *donated* the shirt instead of tossing it in the trash."

Her father huffed in frustration. "My plane leaves early tomorrow morning and there's only one flight. When am I supposed to shop for another shirt? I don't have time."

Jillian watched her mother slowly remove the spoon from the pan and set it down. It was her only show of emotion but she knew that signal well. She wondered if her father did.

"But you just got back from Florida on Thursday, Franklin. I thought you were planning to stay in Kentucky for a while."

Her father lowered his gaze and picked at some invisible lint on his shirt. "There are no decent courses up here. I'm retired. I should be able to play wherever I want."

"I agree. You deserve to play golf wherever you want. Are we moving to Florida permanently?" her mother asked.

"Some day. Not yet," her father said vaguely, avoiding her mother's eyes. "I'll keep using my frequent flyer miles. I'll be back in a week… two at most."

"Do you want me to come down and keep you company? I'm sure you get tired of eating takeout."

"I'm not helpless, Evelyn. No need for all that," her father said, exiting the kitchen before her mother could say anything more to him.

Jillian felt her gut tighten. Her father was constantly leaving her mother behind. Her mother stayed busy in his absence but Jillian never stopped believing it made her mother sad.

Her mother turned back to stir the pan on the stove and sighed in resignation.

"What's wrong?" Jillian asked.

"Nothing. I'm fine. I'm always fine," her mother said.

"I'm sorry, Mama," she said quietly.

Her mother shrugged. "Me too. Franklin's probably seeing

another woman. That's what it usually means when he doesn't want me around."

"What?" Jillian said in surprise. Did her mother suspect her father was having an affair? "Surely Daddy wouldn't cheat on you?"

Her mother laughed. "Girl, he's been doing that forever, but I'm still the one with legal rights. My prenuptial agreement is ironclad. Your father's never leaving me. My mama made sure of that.

"*What?*" Jillian all but yelled, putting a hand to her gut. "Grandma told you to get a prenuptial agreement?"

"Lord, yes," her mother said with a laugh. "She stood next to me while I read and signed it."

"Why would she make you do that?" Jillian demanded.

"Because men are men, Jillian. You gain one pound or get a few wrinkles and they're done with you, especially men your father's age. I'm fine with his flings. She won't last long. None of them ever do. At the end of his life, I'll be the last woman standing at his side. I plan to outlive him."

Stunned by the blunt honesty suddenly dropped on her, Jillian went to sit at her mother's granite island. How could she look at her father now and not feel disgusted? How could she look at her mother and feel anything but sorry for the woman.

"I knew you and Daddy weren't exactly a love match, but Mama, how can you stay with a husband who cheats on you? It's against everything the church teaches, everything you believe."

Her mother barked out a laugh. "I'm forgiving him seventy times seven like scripture says, Jillian. Your father's a good man in most respects and I'm not a stupid girl with dreams. I have a good, solid life. If you'd get your head out of the clouds, you could have a good life too. And you wouldn't have to work so hard."

"I like my work most of the time. Plus, I make good money. I don't need a man for that reason."

"Oh, I know exactly the reason you need a man," her mother said with a sad head shake. "Women your age all got that. But you'll lose that need in a decade and then where will you be? Find a husband while you still want someone sharing your bed. Women who wait too long end up working until they're ninety and living alone until they die."

"How is that different from your situation, Mama. You live alone most the time," Jillian pointed out.

"Are you sassing me?"

"No," Jillian exclaimed, offended by the idea. "I'm asking you questions because the state of my parents' marriage shocks me to the bone. Didn't you and Daddy ever love each other?"

Her mother snorted. "Well, we obviously didn't have whatever pie-in-the sky ideal you keep looking to find. I hope you figure out soon that it doesn't exist like you think it does. That handsome professor at UK could help you just fine with those woman needs of yours. The man will never make as much money as your father, but at least he's your age. That was high up on your marital wish list, wasn't it?"

Jillian shook her head firmly but her mother never turned to see her doing it. "I'm looking for love. I'm looking for what Jackson found."

"You mean an early grave? Your brother certainly found that. Jackson could have been a professional basketball player making all kinds of money if he hadn't gotten seduced by that girl he had no business being around."

"Mama!" Jillian protested.

"Don't Mama me. You need to see how things really are, Jillian. April was nothing but trouble for your brother. Woman didn't even know how to use birth control. They could have stopped at two babies and had a decent life. Jackson might still have made it to the NBA. Instead, they're both in the grave. God only knows what's going to become of their children. All four are going to grow up not even realizing they're not white. Your father and I could have saved two of them from that fate."

The air around Jillian shimmered with anger as her heart threatened to beat its way out of her chest. Her breath was gone. She was going to choke on the bigotry of her parents if she stayed any longer. "I can't listen to any more of this. I really can't. I have to leave."

"Nonsense," her mother said briskly. "Dinner's nearly ready. We'll eat as soon as your father finishes his packing. He's just going to have to make due with his old golf shirts. Jillian? Where are you going? You can't seriously be leaving. A woman your age ought to be a lot tougher than that."

Jillian shook her head as she moved through the house she grew up in on auto-pilot. It took her longer than it should have to find her purse and keys. It was the shock, she knew. It was the epiphany of hearing her worst fears confirmed. Her mother would never understand her feelings—never understand how badly it hurt to know she had not been created from the kind of love she longed to find.

Thank God Jackson hadn't been by her side today. Her brother would have hated their parents for life if he'd heard that discussion. Her brother would have gone home to the woman who loved him and never looked back.

So why didn't she react like that? Instead of hating her father and mother, she just felt destroyed by the shallowness of their lives. She felt betrayed by their lack of love for each other. Why marry at all if being with someone meant so little to you?

Tears slid down her face as she started her car. Her mother was right about one thing though. A woman in her mid-thirties should be able to handle the truth about her family with a lot more poise. She certainly shouldn't be hanging around and wishing for approval. Her parents didn't even share her basic human values.

As she drove away, Jillian realized she had a lot of letting go to do—a lot of letting go.

Blinking at the moisture blurring her vision, she turned the car along familiar streets and wondered what it would be like if she never returned to see her parents.

She also prayed that even if she never found the kind of love Jackson did with April that she'd still one day find something better than the relationship her parents had. She would never, ever stop praying for that.

JOE WAS LOCKING THE BEDROOM DOOR WHEN HIS DOORBELL RANG. Glancing at the clock, he could see it was time for dinner which explained why he was hungry. Deciding to keep whatever mis-delivered pizza was out there, he unfastened the locks on his front door without checking the peephole.

"Jillian," he said in shock. Then, he saw the tears streaking down her face. He took two steps and lifted her chin to search her gaze. "What's wrong? Are you hurt? Did someone attack you?"

Jillian sniffed. "Why is it that's always the first thing guys ask when they see you've been crying?"

Shrugging one shoulder, Joe held her gaze. "We're wired with the instinct to protect," he answered.

Jillian nodded. Okay. She'd give him that. "I wasn't attacked. I found out my father is cheating on my mother. She knows and doesn't care because he's done it many times before. What kind of marriage is that? Not my kind. That's for sure."

Joe scratched his head at the news. What could he say? His parents had fought every day they'd been together. Peace had been a rarity until his father had left. "I think Shane wrote a paper on those kinds of relationships once. Mating rituals was a specialty of his. And marriages used to be primarily about business, politics, and land. Maybe there are pockets of that left in our day and age." He lifted Jillian's cold fingers and warmed them in his grip. "Want to come in and talk about it? I'll listen better now that I know you're not physically hurt."

Nodding, Jillian let Joseph lead her inside his apartment. "What would you do if you found out your wife was cheating on you?"

"Let her go," Joe answered instantly as they walked inside. "My mother hung onto my father long after he lost interest in her. It was bad. That is not a healthy choice for anyone."

Jillian sighed. "Yeah, I'd let her go too. Why be with someone who doesn't want you, right?"

"So you'd let your wife go? I admit I've been wondering a lot about that," Joe teased, taking the smack to his chest in stride. "I'd also probably track down the guy who slept with my wife and cut his balls off so he couldn't do it again. But that's just me. I'm a revengeful bastard. Think a lot of Celtic blood still runs in my veins."

Jillian hung her head. "Can I use your bathroom to wash my face?"

"Sure. Go to the one in the bedroom. It's cleaner."

"You keep an impressively clean bathroom, Joseph McEldowney."

Joe chuckled at the praise. "I change my sheets every week too."

"Then why did I have to do your dishes?"

Joe shook his finger. "That's a low blow. I told you I had a busy week."

Jillian laughed but didn't comment back as she walked away from him. Joe watched her disappear and wondered if she had any idea why she kept running to him when her life got hard. They hadn't seen each other or spoken in weeks and then suddenly she was at his damn door.

What if he'd had a date tonight? It was Saturday after all.

No reason he could come with made any sense in explaining her actions.

But then he'd never really understood how women thought no matter how much he'd cared about one.

JOE WAS RINSING DISHES AND LOADING THE DISHWASHER WHEN Jillian returned to his living room. "Don't give me that side-eye look. I didn't want you worrying about my dishes and doing them after I fall asleep."

"Get out. I was just doing you a favor the other night."

Joe laughed at her rebuttal. "No. A favor is buying the beer at a ballgame or watering my houseplants while I'm out of town."

Jillian looked around. "Well, I might do that but I don't see any plants."

"Because I don't have any," Joe said with chuckle. "I was being rhetorical in my example."

Jillian rolled her eyes and went to sit on the couch. "Don't throw your big words at me tonight, Joe. I'm not in the mood."

Joe grinned. "Okay. Want a glass of wine?"

Jillian turned a blank stare his way and her momentary speechlessness made him laugh again. "You bought wine for me?" she finally said.

Joe nodded. "Yes. I take being chastised to heart."

Jillian closed her eyes and chuckled. "Who would ever believe you were such a sensitive male? Look, I'm sorry I was mean to you the other day. Yes, I'd love a glass of wine."

"Good. I bought two bottles of red wine, an opener, and stemmed glasses. The guy at the store said to go with a Pinot Noir or a Cabernet. I bought both."

"Pinot Noir, please," Jillian said.

"Done. Dinner's on the way too. The chances of us getting the pizza I ordered are slim but the chances of us getting someone else's pizza are extremely good. The place I get pizza from delivers all the pizzas to me no matter who orders in my building. Normally, that's a hassle. Tonight we can just shop the deliveries until we find a pizza you like. I ordered a classic for here in case nothing better shows up."

Jillian shook head as she laughed. "You're trying way too hard to entertain me. Am I making you that uncomfortable?"

"Well, now that you mention it…" Joe carried two glasses of wine to his coffee table and sat down next to her. "I'm babbling because I don't know how to cheer you up. I can't stand to see you cry."

His heart beat loudly when Jillian turned a somber gaze his way.

"You don't have to do anything special. Just seeing you cheers me up. I don't know why since you ignore me to death as well, but that's still the truth."

Joe picked up a wine glasses and handed it to her. "Well, I know why, but you're going to need several more glasses before you're ready to hear my theory."

"Oh, I don't know. Try me," Jillian said with all the bravery she could summon. She held up her wine glass to toast and met his gaze. "To clarity."

Joe touched his glass to hers. "To revelations."

Jillian snickered as she took a sip. "I don't need any more revelations. I got enough from my mother today."

Joe did his best not to make a face over the wine and set down his glass on the table as nonchalantly as he could. He opened his mouth to ask her about her mother but the doorbell rang. One of Jillian's eyebrows went up.

"That was fast. You barely said the word pizza and it's here."

"Not ours," Joe informed her. "The place takes thirty to forty-five minutes on Saturday nights. But hang loose. Let's see what kind it is before we turn it away."

"You're not seriously going to take someone else's pizza, are you?"

"How much clarity do you want from me?" Joe asked as he answered the door. "What kind of pizza is it?" he asked the delivery person.

"Uh…" the kid searched the box. "Pineapple and ham."

Joe turned around and yelled into the apartment. "Interested in pineapple and ham?"

"Not really. Let's hold out for pepperoni and mushrooms," Jillian called back.

"Sorry—not interested," Joe said, turning back to the kid. "What's the apartment number?" The kid looked and recited the one on the box aloud. "Take it two doors down on the right."

Mumbling thanks, the kid hustled down the hall.

Joe closed the door and headed back to the couch and Jillian. He started to sit and the doorbell rang again before his ass successfully touched down. Jillian laughed when he sprung back up and headed to the door again.

"They have at least ten different delivery people. Fridays and Saturdays are busy."

"You need to put a chair outside in the hallway and start

charging for directions," she said.

"Sometimes I do sit out there but I never charge," Joe explained. "I drink beer and watch the pizzas get delivered. It's cheap entertainment."

He heard her laughing and smiled. He opened the door to greet the delivery person. "Hi. What kind of pizza is it?" Joe demanded.

"Uh..." The girl with seventeen eyebrow piercings searched the box for the answer. "Looks like half cheese and half sausage."

"Still holding out for pepperoni and mushrooms," Jillian called out in a wine mellowed voice before he could repeat the pizza type.

Joe looked at the box and saw the apartment number. "Take this hallway all the way to the end. It belongs to the last door on the left."

He closed his front door and headed back to Jillian. This time he didn't even get past his entryway.

"Wait. Wait. Let me get this one," Jillian insisted, pushing by him while Joe laughed.

He crossed his arms and waited while she opened the door.

"Hi," Jillian said in a sultry voice. "What kind of pizza did you bring me?"

When there was no response, Joe trailed to the door to see why. The kid was standing there staring at Jillian's legs with his mouth hanging open.

"Hey, Junior," Joe said loudly. "The lady asked you a question. Pay attention."

"Uh... it's... let me check." The kid searched the box. "It's a classic."

"Does that come with pepperoni and mushrooms?" Jillian asked.

"Yeah. It's got everything," the kid said proudly, "just like you."

"Excellent," Jillian said, lifting the box from the kid's hands. "Pay him, Joseph. I'll get the plates."

Joe chuckled as Jillian all but knocked him aside moving past him with the hot pizza. He pulled out his wallet and handed the kid a twenty and five. "No ogling next time, kid. I'll report you for being disrespectful."

"Yes, sir," the kid said before running away.

Joe grabbed a piece of paper taped backward to the wall. He slapped it on his door and closed it. "Okay. Fun's over. I hung out the sign to let them know my pizza has already been delivered and they needed to search the box for the right apartment."

"Oh, shoot. This one really is ours," Jillian said sadly as she read the box. She was laughing though as she carried plates piled with pizza to the coffee table.

"You sound disappointed that we didn't get to steal someone's pizza order," Joe said.

Jillian shrugged. "It was a fun game while it lasted. I would have taken the first pepperoni and mushroom that showed up —no matter whose it was. We could have re-routed the classic to them to make up for it."

"If shuffling pizzas is your idea of Saturday night fun, you need to get a new life," Joe said as he sat. "I can't wait to buy a house and skip this sort of thing. The delivery people only stop here because I'm the first door they see off the elevator."

Jillian chuckled. "Well, you're a good sport about it. You didn't swear once."

"Oh, I used to swear," Joe replied with a laugh, "but you're a civilizing influence—as most women are on men."

"Philosophize later. Eat your pizza while it's hot," Jillian ordered.

Joe obeyed happily. Jillian looked ten times happier now than she had when she'd shown up at his door. That was enough reason for him to drink wine with her and not get nosy.

HOT UNDER THE COVERS, JILLIAN WOKE IN THE DARK AND BLINKED. She could tell she wasn't in her own bed but had to squint to see that someone was lying next to her. The person was bigger and male—or that was her guess since he smelled like aftershave.

Her hand went to her head. What had she been drinking? Wine didn't usually do this much damage to her. At least she still had her clothes on which told her the guy in bed with her wasn't a jerk.

She fought free of the covers and followed a tiny trail of light to the bathroom. Glancing back, she saw one of the few men she completely trusted sleeping on his side. Everything in her relaxed at the sight of him.

She paused in Joe's bathroom doorway and tried to reason out why. Shaking her head when she failed to solve the puzzle, Jillian went about the business that had woken her and then crept back out to stand beside the bed.

"Joseph," she whispered. She shook his arm but he didn't move. "*Joe*," she said louder. Still nothing though.

She walked back around the bed and sat down where she'd been sleeping. "Guess two bottles of wine weren't a great idea for either of us," Jillian muttered.

She looked over at Joe still sleeping and sighed. She ought to go home but she was tired and didn't want to. She stood again and unzipped her skirt, folding it before dropping it on the floor. She peeled off her blouse and added that to her pile as well. Now she was at least cool enough to sleep.

She squealed a bit when Joe rolled toward her and put his arm across her waist. They were both substantial people and his queen bed didn't leave her any room to escape his grasp. He pushed his nose into her neck and took a deep breath. It sent a shiver of awareness through her.

"Jillian," he said with eyes still closed.

Jillian raised both eyebrows. The man was sound asleep. How did he know who she was?

Joe's lips moving down her neck wrenched a reluctant moan of arousal out of her. The bra she'd left on suddenly felt like a straight jacket against her swelling breasts. Excitement had blood pumping through her. *This...* this was why she'd turned Simba James away and every other male she'd tried to date since Joseph McEldowney had first touched her.

Joe's lips stopped in the curve of her shoulder but one hand moved unerringly to an aching breast. It was like he knew it needed his attention. His grip felt so damn good to her—so good—and necessary.

Her back arched and sent that hand moving lower. It had traveled that trail down her body several times when they were fooling around, but tonight she wanted more.

No, that wasn't honest. She wanted all of him—all of Joe.

She wanted to get to the bottom of why this man turned her on more than others had. Why did doing this feel so right with him when it hadn't felt as right with anyone else?

"Joseph," she whispered as his hand dragged hers between her legs as well. "If you're faking sleep to feel me up, I swear I'm going to kick your ass."

By now, he was using her own hand to torture her. His low masculine chuckle over her fussing sent her girly parts into early ecstasy. To stop him, she evaded his grasp and caught his busy hand firmly in hers before he could use his amazingly talented fingers to drive her the rest of the way to bliss.

Jillian held onto to him with all her might. "Oh, no. We've done enough of that. I want way more from you this time. Give it to me. I know you want to."

"Are you sure?" Joe asked in a rough whisper as he leveraged himself over her and pressed his erection against her thigh.

Jillian couldn't find suitable words to reply so her answer was to wrestle his shirt off and unfasten his pants while he half-groaned and half-laughed at her haste.

Somewhere in their struggle Joe unclasped her bra and latched onto a nipple to slow her down, but Jillian didn't let that heaven stop her.

Removing her own panties, her back arched in desperate relief as Joe finally, finally slid inside her. Her body welcomed him in spasms of joy that required no prompting from his fingers at all. He filled her perfectly. It was hard to say which of them was more surprised.

"Joe," she said in wonder.

She heard him try to say her name as he rose above her. Before she could prompt him to move, Joe surged forward hard. At the same time, he also found her mouth and speared inside it with his tongue.

Then there was no speaking, just lovemaking music as his body played against hers in perfect rhythm. The dance was glorious. Their lovemaking exceeded any dream of sex she'd allowed herself to have about the two of them.

They reached the final peak together straining further into their full connection with faces buried in each other's throats to stifle their groans and screams.

The answers to all her questions were suddenly clear in the silence that descended while their heartbeats fought to return to normal.

She wanted to keep the man inside her.

Forever.

But that would require a complete change of plans.

JOE WOKE WHEN THE PILLOW WHACKED HIM ACROSS THE FACE. HE sat up and blinked hard as his brain fought to catch up. Who was hitting him?

"How could you be like that? I don't fucking believe you," Jillian yelled, standing over him like a vengeful goddess.

"What...?" Joe shook his head to clear it and tried to ask Jillian what was wrong. The pillow hitting him again knocked him flat in the bed before he could ask a real question.

He laughed at her fierceness and snatched the pillow on the next swing. "Is this how you say good morning? No wonder you're not married yet. You're expecting a lot if you think someone ought to tolerate this kind of grumpy ass shit."

Jillian put both hands in her wild hair, squealed indignantly as she pulled handfuls of it, and stomped into his bathroom.

Joe rubbed his face and realized too late that all she'd had on was one of his shirts. The bathroom door slamming made his ears ring and his head pound. He promptly marked red wine off his drinking list because a booze headache was so not worth it. A couple of beers never gave him a headache.

But he ended up laughing again as his head cleared because he had no freaking idea what in the hell had set Jillian off.

He finally managed to pull himself out of bed even though his rubbery legs definitely did not want to cooperate this morning. The woman swearing in his bathroom had proven to be every bit the workout he'd expected.

"It's okay," Joe yelled. "I'll use the other bathroom. When I get back, maybe we can talk about your morning insanity."

"Go to hell," Jillian yelled back.

Joe winced but snickered. As he trekked to the other bathroom, he tried to remember what they'd done last night. That first time inside her had been magical. The other times had been adventurous. He didn't remember leaving her behind at any point, but women were strange.

Waking up to a pillow whopping proved he'd failed as a lover somehow, didn't it?

Joe was putting coffee on when Jillian stumbled out of his bedroom in nearly nothing. She lifted a hand in the air and glared at him.

"You destroyed my bra and I destroyed my underwear. I officially have no clothes to wear home," she complained. "Are you happy?"

"No answer I make is going to sound anything but sexist. However… you can borrow a pair of my sweatpants to wear. We're mostly the same height," Joe said calmly. He pushed the button to start the coffee maker and hoped for the best. "And lucky you—I'm pretty good at fixing things. Maybe I could staple your bra back together. How badly did I damage it?"

Jillian gritted her teeth and made a growling sound. "Staple my bra back together? That's all you have to say about things? Why didn't you tell me this could happen?"

"Tell you what could happen?" Joe asked. He was genuinely

confused, but somehow he didn't think confessing it was going to calm the storm in Jillian.

She muttered "bastard" under her breath and disappeared into his bedroom again. Minutes later she came out wearing some of his dirty clothes that he'd left lying in the floor. He started to tell her where to find clean sweats, but feared for his life.

When Jillian made her way into his kitchen and started rummaging through cabinets, Joe put a hand over one of hers and opened a nearby one. With his free hand, he retrieved a coffee cup with a lid. "Looking for this? I'm feeling kind of desperate for caffeine this morning too."

Jillian glared at him. "You weren't supposed to be like that, Joseph. You were supposed to be average."

Joe pondered multiple meanings which could be applied to the accusation, but eventually gave up. "Just tell me what I did wrong so I can apologize. Whatever it was, I promise you the last thing I ever intended was to make you upset at me. Last night was amazing."

"I know," Jillian all but yelled. "*That's* my fucking problem."

"Sweetie, there's no problem. You have absolutely nothing to worry about. You're a fucking queen in the bedroom and that's not a metaphor or a big word. That's just the honest truth."

"Joe, how could you be like that with me?"

"Like what?" Joe asked in frustration, taking the cup and lid from her limp fingers. "Let's start over, okay? I'll say good morning... then you'll say good morning. Can we at least try for normal? I'll make you pancakes."

"Pancakes?" Jillian saw the man was clueless, but his ignorance didn't change anything for her. Nothing was going to fix what had passed between them.

"Hell," she said as she stepped into him to put her mouth

on his. Unfortunately, Joe tasted as good this morning as he had last night. He fell against her at the first sign of welcome. Her hands had a mind of their own. She stripped him free of his clothes before they'd taken a break from kissing.

His blue eyes changed to deep navy just before Joe groaned and went for her. Next thing she knew his borrowed sweatpants were around her ankles and she was bent over his counter screaming loudly while he made her happy to be a female.

She'd lost all her common sense where he was concerned.

When it was done for her, Joe still hadn't finished. He turned her around in his arms, kissed her senseless until his erection was even harder, and then the idiot swept her up in his arms. She was nearly as tall as he was, and probably didn't way much less, but he practically jogged to the bedroom with her.

Breathing as hard as a racehorse, he threw her down on his bed before ripping the rest of her clothes off and making her see heaven yet another time before he called her name in bliss.

Next time she woke up, Jillian turned her head and found an exhausted Joe snoring deeply beside her. The bedside clock announced it was now past noon instead of early morning. Jillian pulled her well-used body upright and swore again.

Ashamed of her urges and of giving in to them, she scrambled around the bed and floor until she finally found enough clothing to cover her nakedness again.

She fisted hands on her hips as she glared one last time at the man who'd forever changed her idea about what it was like to be wanted. Why did it have to be him?

Damn him. Damn. Damn. And double-damn.

Joe had turned out to be so much more than a great kisser with clever fingers.

13

JOE WOKE MID-AFTERNOON WITH CAFFEINE DEPRIVATION AND MORE male satisfaction than he'd known was possible to feel.

The rest of his Sunday passed in a haze though. Talk about having the mother of all sex hangovers. He poured the coffee he'd made earlier down the sink before noticing the cup and lid he'd given Jillian were missing from the counter. She must have scavenged a cup before leaving.

While he made a fresh pot, he couldn't help wondering if Jillian was feeling as rough as he was. He wondered about other things too.

Had she left even madder at him? Or had she finally calmed?

That last round of sex in the kitchen had pretty much sent him to a physical place he'd never visited before. He'd have told her how spectacular she was if she hadn't run away.

After a restless Sunday night of smelling her on his sheets and still not hearing from her, Monday came despite his resistance to greet another day. Jillian wasn't answering his calls or replying to his texts. Worse, he didn't know where she lived because he'd never asked so he couldn't even send flowers with an apology note. Sure, he could have found the information out from Reesa, but not without confessing their ongoing carnal sins.

Not that Joe was ashamed of anything they'd done—quite the opposite.

Their chemistry was the stuff of romance novels but that had been there since the first day she'd stumbled through Reesa's yard to interrogate Shane. He'd looked down the ladder into her cleavage and lost all interest in seeing anyone's breasts but hers.

Of course he never told her that. How could he? They went to the same bar and he'd seen her with other men who were not like him at all. Not only was he outside the skin color spectrum, in every other way Joe was nothing like all the polished men Jillian dated. They were business men and lawyers and shit—men in suits and shiny shoes. He did good most days to shave and only had one suit to his name.

He was nothing Jillian wanted in a man—that was clear enough. She was fine china and he was a paper plate.

So why had Jillian suddenly made the decision to push the boundary of their relationship? Had it been to get even with her father who was cheating on her mother?

He'd been careful not to set a spark to that mutual lust they had for each other. Jillian had finally struck the match but both of them had been surprised at the amount of flame it produced.

His only regret about any of it was in not knowing how Jillian felt about their time together.

He also had no idea what he'd done wrong in making love with Jillian, but she'd inferred he'd crossed some invisible line. Or at least that was all he could logically conclude from her ranting.

Too bad he couldn't ask for help in discovering the problem.

Instinct told him telling Reesa about them sleeping together would only make things worse.

Jillian's reaction to them having sex was so crazy. One minute she'd been fussing at him and the next she was ripping off his clothes and making all the blood leave his brain.

The whole weekend had been mind-blowing. Now he couldn't stop thinking about her. He couldn't stop wishing she'd come back.

Desperate for a distraction that might keep him from obsessing, Joe left the house and went to hang some gutters.

On Tuesday, he headed to repair someone's deck and worked until dark to finish it in a day.

By Wednesday, he was back in the second bedroom of his apartment working on the torso that was finally coming alive under his hands. He didn't stop working on that piece until his subject was fully formed and looking back at him with inquisitive eyes.

The person he was bringing to life had turned out very differently than he'd planned. Was that some message his subconscious was sending to him? He suspected it was. Maybe Jillian had a right to be mad. He hadn't been careful with her. He'd taken what she offered without regard to proprieties or dating rules. But saying no to her hunger for him? Never happening.

Time alone would tell if his selfishness had any consequences. He just hoped she stopped being mad soon.

After getting some much needed sleep, Thursday afternoon Joe forced himself to shave and put on some clothes without holes in them. He wrapped up several pieces of his art in kitchen towels and stashed them in the smallest duffle he could find in his closet.

Locating a parking place at UK was always a struggle, but

Joe lucked out in finding a metered one in front of the art building. He now had two hours to carry out his plan.

What he was about to do was either brave or more stupid than sleeping with Jillian had been.

AS HE GOT CLOSER, JOE COULD SEE THE MAN WORKING AT HIS DESK. He looked so serious and engaged that Joe hated to interrupt. Before he could turn and sneak away unnoticed, Professor Simba James raised his head and saw him.

"Hi," Joe said, fighting his discomfort at being caught.

Simba waved a hand for him to enter. "Come in, Joseph. I forget your last name, but you're Jillian's friend, right?"

"Yes," Joe said, hoping that was still true. He shuffled from side-to-side in Simba's doorway. "Got a minute or two to talk art with me? And you can just call me Joe."

Simba waved to the chair in front of his desk. "Certainly."

Joe carried his duffle with him and put it on the floor beside the chair as he sat. "I need some artistic help."

"With what?" Simba asked.

Joe reached into the duffle and drew out a statue. He unrolled the man from the cloth and set the statue on Simba's desk. "Do you know any wood carvers? Or anyone who's an expert in African art?"

"I am not a carver of any sort, but I have a trained eye for all mediums." Simba nodded to the statute. "May I?"

"Sure. That's why I came." Joe lifted the carving and placed it in Simba's outstretched hand.

The professor inspected the man from top to bottom, even turning him over to look at the base before he said a word.

"This was carved from very high quality materials. I don't know what tribe is being represented. Perhaps the mysterious

Jim was being obscure about its tribal affiliation on purpose. Many artists do that so they don't get narrowly branded in museums."

"Mysterious Jim?" Joe asked, not understanding.

"The artist put his name on the base," Simba explained, tilting the statue toward Joe so he could see. "See? J.I.M."

"Yes, I do see that," Joe said, feeling sheepish as he nodded. His throat was suddenly dry as dust. He hadn't realized that the initials for Joseph Ian McEldowney spelled a name.

Simba returned to his study of the statue. "Whatever you paid for this was probably worth it. This looks like an early piece. It is slightly flawed with small nicks and tool slips, but visually very powerful nonetheless. The artist's attention to detail is quite extraordinary. You should talk to local artist, William Larson. He works in stone. He can advise you much better than I can about the quality of the design."

"I..." Joe paused and swallowed. The urge to confess was almost unbearable. "Can I show you a few more?"

Simba shrugged as he nodded. "I have reservations for dinner but my date is running behind. We can look at your pieces until she arrives."

Joe pulled out a Bengal Tiger and another statue of a person. This time it was a woman instead of a man. He moved them both within Simba's reach, then returned to the bag to retrieve the rhino. He unwrapped it and set it gently down by the tiger. He had a huge attachment to his first piece and wanted to hear what the art professor thought of it. He waited for Simba to tell him something about the woman, but he was still studying the details on the draped cloth he'd carved on her.

"She's exquisitely done. I have a sense that I know her. Perhaps she reminds me of my own tribe. Art can often evoke deep feelings, even when it..." Simba drifted off in shock as his gaze landed on the rhino. He set down the woman and picked up the rhino. "What do you do for a living, Joe?"

Joe had to clear his throat to speak. "I'm a carpenter by trade."

Simba moved his gaze from the rhino to Joe. "I hope I'm not revealing something unknown to you, but I've actually seen this piece before. It wasn't signed or finished at the time. When I asked about the artist, Will Larson jokingly told me his carpenter made it. I wasn't sure he was even being serious. I see now that he was."

Joe rubbed his forehead. "Will showed my rhino to you? This is so crazy. I feel like I'm either going to throw up or pass out."

Simba laughed. "Please do neither. I don't want to be late for dinner. Carolyn is a very nice woman. Jillian introduced us. I think they both work at the same place."

"I don't get it. You're a great guy. Why didn't you and Jillian date? You two seemed a perfect match."

Simba shrugged. "We did date, but not seriously. I got the distinct impression that she was interested in someone else."

Joe swallowed hard. "I've never gotten that. Did she ever say who he was?"

"Not a word," Simba said. Then he smiled. "Now I am more fascinated that it was you I met that evening. I believe our destinies were meant to cross."

Joe's mouth lifted in a small smile. "You sound like Shane. Will's son and I have been best friends for years. He believes in all that woo-woo stuff."

"Woo-woo stuff," Simba repeated. "Your comment makes me mourn the loss of magic in the world."

Joe shrugged. "I tend to have that effect on a lot of people who meet me."

Simba chuckled and tapped his desk to hold Joe's attention.

The man kept looking away. "What you are feeling is just artistic nerves, Joe. You must get used to being put on the spot by those viewing your work. Are you African in heritage?"

"Not even a tiny bit," Joe admitted uncomfortably. "My family all came from Ireland."

"You are Celtic? They would be appalled by your attitude toward woo-woo stuff, as you call it. Why do you think you have such a large fascination with African art?"

Joe pondered his answer but in the end settled on the truth. He was tired of hiding it. "I'm in love with an African American woman. She doesn't love me back. I don't fit her plans."

"She's your inspiration though, isn't she? You're trying to understand her through your art," Simba concluded.

Joe thought about it before nodding reluctantly. "Before meeting her, I never gave anyone's race or color any real thought. I don't even understand why that matters. You'd think our world would be more accepting of differences, especially in America. I think we still have a ways to go."

Simba smiled and turned the statue of the woman to face Joe. "This is a proud, confident female you have carved. I can't help but be curious about what she might possibly fear. Are your families in the way of your love?"

Joe nodded as he stared at the first version he'd ever made of Jillian. It wasn't great and it wasn't her. Only a slight likeness was there. "Our parents are the only real problem. If she could get over caring about keeping peace in her family, I'd shout my feelings about her to the world."

Simba pushed the woman back to Joe. "I think you already are shouting your feelings to the world—at least the small part of the world that has seen these pieces. Just how loud were you thinking of being? You might talk to Carrie Larson about doing a show at her gallery."

Joe drew in a breath and released it slowly. "I guess my loudness level was going to depend on what the professional opinion was about my work."

"What makes me a professional? My art degree? Will has no art degree and I seek his opinion all the time. In the bigger sense, my opinion is nothing. All I can say is that you did a nice job with the details," Simba said with a wave. "The best kind of art is not about perfection, but about what each person feels when they view it. That's what African art is meant to convey—pride, joy, connection, family—just to name a few things. All that is in your work, Joe."

"Thanks, Simba," Joe said sincerely. "I owe you."

"Good," Simba said with a smile. "I will collect. I need some bookcases made for my house."

"Done," Joe said. "You pick the materials and I'll build them for free."

"Excellent. Today is a very good day," Simba said.

Joe nodded but instantly thought of the one thing that would make it much better.

JOE WALKED INTO THE GALLERY JUST AS CARRIE WAS LOCKING UP.

"Hey Joe," Carrie said. "I was packing up for home. Look, I know I owe you those sizes for the walls but I haven't been able…"

"It's not that. I'm here about something else," Joe said. He lifted the duffle. "I have some things to show you if you have just a bit of time. They're small. It won't take long."

Carrie stopped as her eyes fell on the duffle. "Sure." A cautious smile lifted the corners of her mouth. "Let's go into the conference room. You're being very mysterious."

"Mysterious is my other name. You can call me Jim."

"Why? Are you changing your name?" Carrie asked with a laugh.

"I may have to in order to get through this," Joe said as he pulled the rhino from the duffle and handed it over. "I may have found you that cache of exclusive African art you were hoping for."

Carrie's eyes widened as she took the polished piece into her hands. "Wow. This is fantastic. Look at the details on his feet. I can even make out his toenails. And the eyes are wonderful." She turned the piece over. "JIM," Carrie read with a laugh and then immediately sobered. "Who's Jim?"

Joe blew out the breath he'd been holding before speaking. "Jim is Joseph Ian McEldowney—those are my initials."

"*You* made this piece?" Carrie looked back down at the rhino in shock. Her heart thumped in excitement. "Have you created any more like this?"

"Yes. Forty some pieces I think," Joe said softly. "I haven't really counted. I've been working on bigger ones lately." He unwrapped the statues of the man and woman. "Half are this size. The animals are smaller."

Carrie drew in a breath as she lifted them. "How big is the biggest one?"

"The one I'm working on now would only fit on the largest pedestal I made you. It's more involved."

Carrie eyes sparkled as showcase possibilities bloomed in her mind. "Are you interested in selling any of these?" she asked as casually as she could.

Joe shrugged. "I don't know. Maybe. I never got that far in my thinking. I just wanted..." He stopped and sighed. "I want to show these to the world. I figure you'd know how I could do that."

"Anything off-limits?" Carrie asked.

"The rhino," Joe said instantly. "It was the first piece I finished. I'd show it but it's never going to be for sale."

"Completely understandable," Carrie said with a wave of her hand over it.

Joe swallowed, fighting the knot of tension in his throat. "And I don't think I can sell the big piece I'm working on either. I'd maybe consider leaving it in the gallery on permanent display or something. I have no place at home for it."

"In that particular case, I'd rent your artwork on contract so my insurance would cover it," Carrie said, putting a hand on Joe's wrist. She could feel him shaking under her touch. "Joe, what are you nervous about? Surely, you realize that your work is fantastic. I'm so glad you brought it to me. I'm honored. We'll come up with a name and plan for a showing."

"African Dreams," Joe said without thinking. Simba might like knowing Joe used his description. "I'd like to call it that if you think it works. I have pieces that are not African, but this was my first creative obsession."

"African Dreams. Yes, I like that name. Consider it done," Carrie said. "Who else has seen your work besides me?"

"Will gave me lessons and made me keep going. I told Shane a couple weeks ago. And today I took these to Professor James at UK for an educated opinion, but I found out Will had already done that. He saw the rhino before it was finished."

Carrie smiled. Artistic journeys and their synchronicities never surprised her. She seen them happen too often. "So what did Simba have to say about your work?"

"He said to bring it to you if I wanted the world to see it, but…"

"But what?" Carrie asked cheerfully. There was always a "but" for first-timers. Her specialty was in resolving them.

"Can we not tell anyone who I am? I'm not sure I'm ready to…"

"Be declared an artist?" Carrie asked. "Because you're not going to be able to control anyone's reaction when they look at your work. Some people are going to say that being a white male in a privileged country that you have no business carving things you know nothing about. Writers are told that all the time when they dare write about something outside their daily lives. But that's not how the imagination works. That's not how creativity works. Art manifests through whatever individual it wants to."

Joe closed his eyes. "But I'm not a Larson, Carrie. I don't think I have enough rebel in me to be an artist. Even Will looking at my work makes me ill."

"Joe, I hate to tell you this, but that's normal for artists."

"Well, fuck that shit," Joe said with great sincerity.

Carrie laughed, not the least offended by his passionate reaction. "I think you have way more bravery than you realize, but we can keep your identity quiet for a short time. The mystery might help draw in a larger crowd. It's only fair to warn you though—anonymity doesn't last long in today's excessive information world," Carrie said.

Joe nodded. "Right. I can see that." Hadn't he also decided that he was done hiding his feelings? "I'll deal with it once it comes to light. Hopefully, I won't barf on the person who figures it out or punch them."

"You'll be fine. "Can I keep everything but the rhino?"

Joe nodded. "Sure. I guess so. If you want."

"And will you come by tomorrow and sign a contract so I can get started on the promotion of your work?"

Running a suddenly shaking hand over his hair, Joe nodded again. "I suppose I can do that too. Are you sure about showing my work?"

"Yes, I'm sure, Joe. And I'll have the measurements for my portable walls by the time I see you too. I want to get them done before you get too busy to do them. Good carpenters are hard to find in this town. You being a friend of Michael's and his family was like a gift from god. I should have known it wasn't going to last."

Her comment made him laugh, but nothing was calming the butterflies in Joe's stomach. "You're sure you're not just…"

Carrie narrowed her gaze and shook her head slowly and deliberately. "If I wasn't completely sure, I would have told you the pieces were good but not great yet. I would have sent you back home with your art to improve your skills. I am sure I can sell these pieces. If the rest is as good as these, you and I are going to be business partners until you get too big for my gallery."

"Michael is a lucky man. You're damn good at ego stroking," Joe said.

"I'm damn good at selling art too," Carrie promised. "Bring me more, mysterious JIM. I'll do the rest."

Joe nodded at her determination. Carrie's gaze only dropped from his when her phone buzzed with a message. "Reesa went into labor early. They're prepping her for an emergency C-section now. Michael left Ivy with Jessica. Ellen's watching the rest of the kids. Let's go before Shane has a meltdown."

"Can I drop you at the hospital?" Joe asked.

"Yes. Michael drove me today," Carrie said, chuckling when Joe hastily set a series of animals on the table next to the people. "He likely doesn't realize I'm stranded here. Seeing Shane stressed is all the worry he can handle."

She grinned when Joe carefully rolled the rhino back up in one of the towels and returned it to the duffle.

"Joe, I don't think I've been this excited about a showing since I featured Shane's drawings of Reesa. Thank you for bringing your work to me. I promise you that I'm going to make you glad you did."

Joe made a face. "I hope you're still saying that when someone offers you two dollars for that Bengal tiger and ten for the two statues together."

"Joseph, Joseph—you have so much to learn," Carrie said as they headed out the door.

14

THE HOSPITAL WAS BUZZING WITH ACTIVITY. JOE FOUND SHANE IN the waiting room with his face in his hands.

"Heard you're about to be a daddy," Joe said brightly.

"She was home by herself when her water broke. She called Mom to come get Sarah. Brian was at soccer practice. Chelsea was tutoring. She'll pick up Brian when they're done. Zach's away at a game. Dad and Jessica were in Cincinnati. They're on their way home."

Joe's eyes widen at the logistical recitation. He stood next to his giant friend and rubbed his back which was seventeen kinds of tense. "So everything's covered then, right?"

"She wasn't supposed to have labor, Joe. She wasn't supposed to have pain. That's why we planned a C-section when we found out how big the baby was going to be."

"I'm sure Reesa's going to be fine," Joe said. "Women are warriors when it comes to childbirth. Your wife is one of the toughest women I know."

"She's been in labor for hours now. They weren't able to stop it," Shane said.

Jillian walked into the room and Joe fought not to stare. She looked really good and he wanted badly to kiss her. She met his gaze briefly then moved on to the expectant father.

"Well, what did you expect, Shane. The woman's giving birth to a big old shaggy Viking baby. I heard it could be twelve pounds."

"Twelve pounds? Wow, that's a huge kid," Joe exclaimed, then he met Shane's troubled gaze. He rubbed harder. "But I'm sure Reesa's going to be just fine."

Jillian huffed. "Of course, she's going to be fine. I just talked to her. They've given her something to make her high. That pre-op shit is good stuff, let me tell you. She demanded to know if it was a boy or girl, but I held strong and didn't tell her."

"It's okay, Jillian. We both know it's a boy," Shane said. "Joe told."

"Joseph! Tell me you didn't do that. Can't you keep a secret?"

Joe winced. Yes, he thought, just not that one. "Sorry, Jillian. Shane made me mad and it slipped out. I was fussing at him for insinuating that his wife was hormonally crazy just because Reesa asked me to get Shane out of her hair for a while."

"Shane Larson! Your wife was never once hormonally motivated in her entire pregnancy. She was just tired of your hovering," Jillian stated loudly, glaring at the worried man.

Shane lifted his shoulders. "She was unreasonable all the time and refused to take care of herself. It's a documented condition of pregnancy."

Jillian rolled her eyes and Joe laughed. He pointed at Shane. "For the last two months, I've been having trouble deciding whether to deck him or hug him."

Shane glared at them both. "They ran me out here to wait while they prep her for surgery. I'm going to be in there. They're not doing anything to her without me."

Jillian went over and sat by Shane's side. She hooked her arm through his. "Girlfriend is going to be just fine. She's out of pain and they're hustling to keep anything from happening until the doctor frees up. There's only one delivery ahead of her."

"I should never have gone to work today," Shane said.

"Oh, hush now. Women go through this all the time. She's going to be fine. You'll see."

Shane nodded and leaned his head against Jillian's.

"Mr. Larson?" A nurse asked at the doorway.

Shane stood up and knocked both Joe and Jillian away in the process. "That's me."

The nurse looked him up and down. "They'll be taking her back in a few minutes. I hope we have some scrubs to fit you. Come with me."

Joe and Jillian both shook their heads as Shane followed quietly behind the nurse.

"God help Reesa. No telling what she's going to say to him with all those drugs in her."

"God help the doctor. If Reesa even so much as moans, Shane's going to deck him. Then he'll get kicked out. Michael isn't allowed on the floor until the baby comes. They remember him from when Ivy was born."

They looked at each other and burst out laughing. After a minute of mutual hysteria, Joe went to sit down in the space Shane had vacated. Jillian looped her arm through his and put her head on his shoulder. Joe turned and kissed her forehead.

"Are we okay?" he asked.

"Yes. Why wouldn't we be?" Jillian asked.

Joe opened his mouth to list the possibilities he'd compiled since the weekend then changed his mind.

"No reason," he said calmly. "Just checking. When you left the other day, I thought maybe you were mad at me. If you ever do get mad at me, I hope you'll give me the chance to apologize before condemning me to hell. I've never been an expert on women and I'd hate to hurt your feelings being my typical dense male self."

Jillian squirmed a little in her seat but tightened her grip on his arm. Joe smiled at her action. That told him everything important.

"I was never mad at you. I was mad at myself for being stupid about you. You could say I was venting."

"Venting?" Joe asked. "Is that like yelling? Because it sounded like yelling."

"Yes. It was emotionally charged yelling which allowed me to express my passionate nature in a safe way with a safe person," Jillian supplied.

"Shane couldn't have said that any better. Express yourself. I got it. Next time I'll know," Joe said, testing the waters.

"Don't worry. I'll remind you," Jillian answered so quietly that he barely heard her.

Joe chuckled and relaxed into the moment. "I'm sorry I told Shane about the baby. He was talking smack about his wife and I lost it."

"You're forgiven, Joseph McEldowney, defender of irrational women."

"You talking about Reesa?" Joe asked in surprise. "But I thought you said…"

Jillian laughed. "Girlfriend is beyond crazy, but that's Shane's fault. He's the one that knocked her up."

Joe chuckled. "So he should suffer?"

"Reesa's had to suffer for nine months carrying a big old Viking baby inside her. It seems only fair."

Grinning, Joe turned and put his arm across Jillian and hugged her close. "God, I lo…" He froze. Had she heard him?

Jillian sighed and slipped her free arm across his waist. "Don't. Just don't. Not today," she ordered.

Joe nodded against her head not sure of what he was agreeing to. Her commands weren't a denial really. They were more of a postponement.

At least, that was the story Joe was going to keep telling himself.

∽

WHEN JUDE EVERETT LARSON FINALLY MADE HIS APPEARANCE, HE weighed in at an enormous 11 pounds and 14 ounces. He nursed practically as soon as he arrived and then went to sleep in the arms of his continuously weeping father. This was the same father who was now asleep on the edge of the hospital bed that Jude's tiny mother was confined to until her anesthesia wore off.

Jillian told him Reesa had named her son after the brother she lost long ago. Shane had added in Will's middle name because it was obvious the boy was going to be another giant Larson male.

"Good Lord," the nurse exclaimed when she walked in and saw no less than ten people crowded into the room. Joe laughed at her shock over how quiet everyone was being so the exhausted new mom and dad could catch a bit of a nap.

Michael had taken Ivy for a walk to wear her out because she wouldn't stop squealing *"bebee bebee"* in Jude's ear every time she got close. Like her father, she was very passionate and that seemed especially true when it came to her new cousin.

A nearly ready to pop Brooke had snuck in after her night class to briefly hold her new nephew. She'd watched her weight and with her larger height no one really would have guessed she was over eight months along. Jillian was taller than Brooke and would probably carry a child like that as well, Joe thought as he watched Brooke cooing over Jude.

Blake had eventually come and gone too, as had Chelsea from her night job and Brandon from a late class.

Zach was coming straight to the hospital after his bus returned from an away game. He'd miss seeing the baby but his real concern was about how his aunt and uncle were faring.

Brian and Sarah were both busy drawing, unconcerned with anything but the art they were creating. Each seemed completely absorbed in what they were doing. Joe wondered if Michael and Shane had been that way as child artists. He couldn't imagine either of them being so quiet or so still. Even as an adult, Shane had the energy of two people.

He didn't know where Ellen's husband Luke was, but Ellen and Will were sitting side by side smiling at everyone in the room.

Sighing, Jessica had professed to be too restless for the group and was walking the hospital hallways. Joe was sure she was nervous because in less than a month her daughter Brooke would be going through this same thing—sans C-section hopefully. But natural childbirth carried its own challenges.

Joe smirked as he noted that baby Jude had yet to be laid in the crib that the hospital had provided. Everyone had taken a turn holding him, but somehow he always ended back up in Auntie Jillian's arms.

His heart compressed at the sight of Jillian holding the infant against her beautiful breasts. No wonder women got painted and portrayed so often as mothers. Jillian holding the child was one of the most beautiful scenes he'd ever witnessed with his eyes.

And that's when it hit him. The vision was suddenly clear and strong and perfect and compelling and... he had to go.

"I have to leave," Joe leaned closer to whisper. "Do you need anything before I go?"

"Thanks—I'm good. They're going to run us all off soon anyway. Visiting hours end at nine for anyone not family."

Joe chuckled low. "Hope they have fun figuring out who's not family with the Larsons and they better hope Shane stays asleep for that debate."

Jillian giggled at his comment. He wanted to kiss her smiling lips but didn't. Instead, his hand went to her cheek without even realizing what he'd done. He smiled and leaned forward to kiss her forehead. "I'll see you later, Auntie Jillian."

"You just might," Jillian whispered back.

Joe stood and waved to the rest of the quiet people in the room before slipping out the door.

15

"HERE'S A SUGGESTED PRICE LIST I DEVELOPED FOR THE PIECES YOU left with me. This is just an example. I'm still researching. If you feel strongly that I'm not pricing competitively enough, we can talk about what numbers make you feel more comfortable."

Joe stared at the sheet of paper in front of him. His shock was complete. "You honestly think these are worth hundreds of dollars each?"

"Yes. And the larger pieces will be worth thousands. If these are one of a kind..."

"They are," Joe said quietly.

"Then we might get some competitive bidding on people's favorites."

Joe scrubbed a hand over his face. "Can you explain this to me? Because I don't get it. I didn't grow up an artist. I don't understand why people would pay so much for my work."

"African artists—those already popular—tend to replicate their bestselling work. This seems like both common sense and a smart financial decision at first. However, replicas automatically lower values. Scarcity and uniqueness makes each piece far more interesting to collectors and art lovers. If I can interest museums in your work, all prices will quadruple in the future. Museums will pay big bucks because they will insist on getting a piece that is uniquely theirs."

Joe lifted both hands. "It just never occurred to me that what I was creating was anything but something that might look okay on a bookshelf or a side table. I tried to give Will the rhino to keep but he wouldn't take it. He just laughed and told me that I needed to hang on to the first piece for the memories."

Carrie chuckled. "Nearly all real artists feel just like that, Joe. That's why I'm glad you brought your art to me. I promise you, I'm going to be worth my third of what I make for you. I can't wait to tear into those boxes you brought me and see what you've got. Did you empty out your stash?"

Joe shook his head. "No. I kept a few to fix some things I saw wrong as I was packing. I'll bring them to you eventually if you want them."

"I'm contractually ready to promise you that I do," Carrie said. Her lips lifted in a smile. "I'm also going to require that I get first choice on future pieces for at least two years. So don't be thinking you're going to take anything to the Smithsonian without me."

Chuckling at the bizarre idea of anything he'd carved being in any sort of famous museum, Joe rolled his eyes. "I promise you I'm not worried about losing out on a deal."

"Bet next time we talk contracts you're going to feel a lot differently." Carrie pushed the contract across the table. "Want to get Luke or somebody to go over it with you before you sign?"

"No, maybe next time—when I've become a prima donna," Joe said with a laugh, playing her game as he signed the papers in from of him.

"Buy a new suit, Joe. You've got a month. I'm going to send

out some photos to garner early interest and start advertising next week." Carrie slid a check across the table. "Here's some good faith money. I try to keep my artists working."

Joe lifted the check and stared at all the zeros. Ten thousand was as much money as he usually made in two months of steady work. This check was not getting cashed. He looked at Carrie. "You can't honestly think we're going to make big money like this on my art."

"Take your original 40 pieces with opening bids ranging between 500 and 1000 each. Calculate your two-thirds of it based solely on beginning bids and you have a small idea of the possible income stream. Even if the smaller pieces end up going for less than I hope, we're still going to make more than you can imagine."

"How can you know this?" Joe asked.

"Mostly because I'm really good at what I do and I love selling art. I've sent emails to several galleries I know who are looking for original African art to showcase just like I've been. There just aren't a lot of genuine artists making it and none I've seen have your eye for detail. Some of the galleries have promised me a healthy deposit just to get first selection before your work goes public. It seemed only fair to share some of that deposit money with you to prove my faith. Maybe building my portable walls is the last carpentry work you'll ever do."

Joe laughed at the idea of giving up all his contracting work. "It won't be. I promised to build Simba James some bookcases."

"Your call, but I suggest you scale back to focus on your art instead," Carrie said lightly, grinning as she gathered up the papers. "When can I see some bigger pieces?"

"Want something not African?"

"Sure. That shows your versatility. Bring me everything."

Joe nodded. "Okay. I'll drop them by tomorrow."

"Perfect," Carrie said.

JOE WAS WRAPPING UP A CARVING OF A LARGE WINGED HAWK native to Kentucky when his doorbell rang. He closed his bedroom door on the way to answer the summons. A smile lit his face as he peered through the peephole.

He opened the door and leaned in the doorway to fully enjoy the picture she made. The burnished dark gold dress with tribal designs on the hem hugged her luscious curves. Both her lip gloss and her heels matched in color. He looked Jillian up and down and felt a male ownership that was becoming less and less foreign to him.

"Lady, you sure know how to package all that heat you're carrying. I get hard just seeing you. I always have."

Jillian swallowed nervously at the bold declaration. His words made her blush but also instantly primed her for the sensual onslaught his gaze promised was coming.

"Let me in, Joseph, before I melt in your hallway."

Joe smiled and held the door open.

"Sorry I didn't bring dinner this time," she said.

"It's okay. I'll make us dinner later," Joe said closing the door. "Unless you're hungry now."

Jillian stopped in the middle of the room. "I'm okay. I can wait on food."

Joe walked closer. "Is that your subtle way of saying that you're hungry for me instead?"

Jillian narrowed her gaze on his grin. "It's a damn admission and you know it—one I'm not comfortable making, so don't go teasing me about it."

Laughing, Joe slipped his arms around her and ran his fingers possessively over her hips. They inspired him to do so many wicked things to her. He kissed her cheek, her temple, and then dipped to her lips to rid her of the lip gloss. Jillian's heat enveloped him until he lost all sense of anything but her.

When he lifted his head, he took Jillian's chin in his fingers to make sure she couldn't look away. "I love you. Before this goes any further, you need to know that. I'm tired of feeling it and not saying it. You're the only woman I've ever felt this way about so it's important to me."

Jillian closed her eyes and sighed deeply. "You have to make this so damn complicated, don't you?"

"Sweetheart, this got complicated the first time I kissed you. The rest was nature taking its course. I know I'm not your ideal male, but sometimes life doesn't work out like we planned. I'd like nothing better than to make you scream my name for the rest of our lives. Loving you and being with you feels like my destiny."

"Destiny," Jillian giggled. "You sure like your fancy words."

"I do, but I *love* my fancy woman. I love her style, her grace, her loving nature, her generosity in bed, and her sense of humor. The only thing I don't love is her tendency to use pillows as a weapon. I'm still unclear if she's issuing a challenge or communicating ineffectively."

Throwing her head back, Jillian laughed. "I swear that was just a momentary thing. I was just so confused about you. The pillow was handy."

Joe shrugged. "Maybe I can clear up your confusion in the next few minutes. I'm looking damn forward to trying."

"No way in hell is sex going to do it," Jillian said firmly. Then she laughed. "But kiss me anyway. I've been thinking about you all week. I've been thinking about you doing a lot of things to me, but let's start with a kiss."

Joe grinned at her confession, but took his time in seducing her. He kissed her and undressed her, leaving a trail of clothes from the living room to the bedroom. By the time they got to the bed, she'd undressed him too.

"I love you," he said, making her his as she wrapped her gloriously long legs around him.

He told himself not to worry when she never said it back.

JOE MADE OMELETS A COUPLE HOURS LATER WHICH THEY ATE sitting on the couch. He'd loaned Jillian a pair of sweats and a t-shirt so she wouldn't have to completely get dressed.

Jillian suddenly stopped eating to pick up the rhino he'd accidentally left out on the coffee table. Startled by his oversight, Joe drew in a breath and waited to hear what she said about it.

"Where did you find this? He's amazing. I love African art. All the pieces I have are mass produced. This one doesn't look anything like my stuff. You can see his toenails. Did you notice that?"

Joe cleared his throat. It was time. "I made him."

"You made this rhino?" Jillian repeated in shock.

Shrugging, Joe nodded. "I took up carving as a hobby. Will gave me lessons."

"Pretty damn good lessons," Jillian said as she studied the details again. She set the rhino back down on the coffee table and began eating again. "You need to keep doing that kind of work. Make me one. I'd love to have something as nice as that."

Joe chuckled at her request. Now he had to read the damn contract he'd signed to see if he could make anything for anyone without Carrie getting a cut.

"Sure," he answered, assuming the best. "What kind of animals do you like?"

"Exotic ones—tigers, elephants, giraffes, *rhinos*," Jillian answered, pointing at the stature on the table. "My mother's roots are from the Republic of Ghana in West Africa. My father's people originally came from Ethiopia which is on the complete other side of the continent. If history had played out differently for my great-grandparents and my grandparents, my parents would likely never have met. I actually think about that a lot since I discovered their marriage has always been a sham. Part of me thinks it might have been better for everyone if they had stayed apart."

Joe shook his head. "You can't go there in your thoughts and make it work out. I know history can be a painful burden. Celts have been historically quick to make hot-tempered mistakes. But think of all that would be erased in both our lives if your ancestors had never met. You and Jackson wouldn't have been born. All your brother and April's amazing children wouldn't be here. You and Reesa wouldn't have met. Shane and Reesa wouldn't have met. I regret what your grandparents and parents may have suffered in their lives, but I get selfish when I've got you wrapped around me, Jillian. I don't want to feel anything but gratitude that we get to happen because they lived through what they did. I am grateful to anyone past or present who makes us possible."

"I hear what you're saying, but Jackson and April did not have an easy life, Joe. People stared at them and at their children. People whispered behind their backs. Zack and Chelsea got picked on for being bi-racial. Brian hasn't had it so bad, but he's so full of attitude that I think he enjoys it. Princess Sarah just hasn't run into it yet at her age. Don't get me started on what people have said about me and Reesa being best friends for all these years. We didn't get shit often, but we did get shit. The struggle is real when you choose to be color-blind to race in your life."

Joe glanced at Jillian and smirked. "How do you know the

shit you got was about race? You have to admit that you too do look pretty funny together. You're over a foot taller than her—probably more in your heels. It's a hard thing not to notice that huge difference in your heights. I'm not surprised people give you two shit."

Jillian snorted and smacked Joe's arm. "You joke, but the struggle to get past color is still real. It's going to take a long damn time for that to change in this country."

Joe nodded. "Doesn't mean you need to put your life on hold or turn away love and friendship."

"No, it doesn't... and I haven't," Jillian said. "But it does make life a bit harder from day to day."

Joe nodded. "I can't disagree, but sweetheart, if people started staring at us, it would be because they were looking at how fine you look. They'd be wondering what in the hell a woman like you was doing with a scruffy man like me. The color difference would be the second thing they wondered about."

"Yeah—you're probably right about that," Jillian said, squealing when Joe went to pinch her. "Stop. I don't mind you looking scruffy. You know I like your man shit or I wouldn't be here."

"Man shit?" Joe asked.

Jillian nodded. "Reesa and I call it that. It's all the shit a man makes you put up with just because he's good to you in bed."

"Huh..." Joe said, considering it. "Shane must be even more incredible than he brags about being. Reesa puts up with a lot."

Jillian fell back against the couch laughing. "You aren't kidding, but she loves that big old Viking more than I thought she could ever love anyone. She always had a ton of guys in her life but not a one of them was like him. And you know what? Reesa was right. Man shit and all, Shane's still worth it."

"Am I worth it to you?" Joe asked.

Jillian's smile faded. "You know you are, but it's going to take me a while to get there. I know you deserve an answer to my waffling. I'm working to turn loose of my previous promises to myself."

Joe was disappointed but he also saw what she struggled with. "I understand. I just hope you get there before the kids start coming along. We need to have our own shit straight before we start helping them with theirs."

Children? Jillian's eyes widened. Astounding sex evidently could distract even the most careful woman in the world. She counted backwards to her last shot of birth control. She needed to check her calendar. "You're serious, aren't you?"

Having injected enough reality into their relationship for one day, Joe decided to use Jillian's favorite tactic and avoid the rest. "I'm going to head to the kitchen and load the dishwasher before I get too tired to do it. Can I get you anything else?"

"A clearer mind," Jillian said.

"Sorry, I'm all out of clear minds," Joe answered. "You'll have to pick one up on your way home."

16

SHE DELIBERATELY STAYED AWAY FROM HIM FOR A COUPLE OF WEEKS, texting her excuses about how busy she was. Joe answered her texts, professing to understand, but the man wasn't stupid. He damn well knew she was avoiding him.

The nausea she'd felt for several mornings straight made her realize that her secret relationship was taking a stressful toll on her digestive system even though almost no one knew about it yet.

Her mother had left voice mails and had texted her. She'd made excuses to her as well. She wasn't ready to hear more of how her father was a good man. She might never see him that way again.

Her endo check-up rolled around on the calendar and she took the whole day off. Maybe if she did something fun it would chase away this fog she seemed to be living in.

She redressed after all the tests were done and was sitting in the exam room. The doctor came in and smiled at her.

"I don't think you've ever smiled at me before. Is the endo gone?" Jillian asked.

"No, it's not gone, but the fibroids have stopped growing. Some even look like they're shrinking. That's good news, Jillian, and congratulations, by the way."

Jillian laughed. "Thanks. I'd like to take credit, but I have no idea what I did to improve my situation. Maybe my body decided to fight back on its own."

"Well, the baby is probably helping the most. From the ultrasound, it looks like you're a couple months along. Is that about right?"

"The what?" Jillian asked as her jaw dropped. How long ago was her last period? "Are you sure I'm having a baby?"

Her doctor laughed and stared in surprised. "Yes. Didn't you intend to? I figured you'd taken my advice."

"No. I had no idea. My last birth control shot was…"

"Jillian, the last time you got a birth control shot was more than 8 months ago. It stopped working at 6 months and I took you off of it on purpose. Remember? It was making the endo worse. Are you saying you had unprotected sex and got pregnant accidentally?"

"Well, I…" Jillian blinked rapidly. Now the dizziness and nausea made sense. It wasn't stress after all. Oh good Lord, she was pregnant with Joe's baby. "Holy shit. I did this to myself."

"If you didn't plan it, you could always…"

"No, no, no," Jillian said, stopping him. She didn't even want to hear that option. "I'm crazy about the guy. I just wasn't…"

"Necessarily planning to have his child?" her doctor filled in.

Jillian nodded. "I always thought women who got pregnant without knowing it were just making that story up. My life has been crazy lately. I can't believe I didn't figure it out."

Her doctor laughed again. "Well, sometimes that's the case, but not often. Sometimes life gets complicated. Six or seven weeks along is still early. Sometimes there are no signs. Babies sneak up on couples all the time."

"Somebody sneaked up on me alright." Jillian ran a hand through her hair. She was going to need to get it cut a lot shorter before the baby came. There'd been no more long hours in the salon.

She also needed to schedule maternity leave from work and find a two bedroom apartment.

And most of all, she needed to tell Joseph that he was going to be father. After all the sex they had, the man was never going to buy any story that it wasn't his. Knowing him, he'd haunt her for the whole pregnancy and then demand a DNA test the moment it was born.

And why in the hell would keeping his child from him even cross her mind? What awful game was she playing with herself? If she kept this up, she was going to need counseling.

"Jillian?" Her doctor snapped his fingers to get her attention. "You okay? I'm sorry you didn't know. If you're going to carry this child to term, let's schedule an obstetrics appointment and get your pregnancy mapped out so you can make some plans."

"Sure."

"I can do the delivery if you like."

Jillian nodded. "That sounds fine to me. You know all my history."

"Are you sure you're okay? You're a little glassy-eyed."

Laughing, Jillian shook her head. "I'm going to be fine. This was just a surprise. It changes things."

"Babies always change things," he said.

"So does falling in love with the last person you ever expected to fall in love with," Jillian replied.

Her doctor nodded as he laughed.

~

"MAMA? ARE YOU HOME?" JILLIAN CALLED AS SHE WALKED INSIDE.

"Jillian? I'm in the kitchen."

Always in the kitchen, Jillian thought. Her mother was always in the kitchen cooking for somebody. Is that what gave her mother's life without love a sense of purpose?

Her mother walked to hug her. "I'm so glad you're here. I was so worried when you didn't call me back. I shouldn't have said anything to you that day. I dishonored your father and myself. What goes on between a man and woman is between them and God."

"Do you really think that way? Or is that just what you're telling me?" Jillian asked.

"That's a strange question," her mother replied.

"Is it?" Jillian asked, taking a seat at her mother's island. "I'm still upset. I'm still in shock that my parents don't love each other. I think it's a very reasonable question."

"There you go making it all complicated when it's not. Your father's coming home early tonight. When I told him about your reaction, he was straightway regretful. He said he was intending to mend his household when he got back."

"But he's been gone the whole two weeks anyway," Jillian pointed out. "Does that sound like a repentant man to you? It doesn't to me. You know he's been with her."

Her mother waved it off. "What does it matter? He's had a change of heart. That's all I need to know."

"Do you honestly think so?" Jillian asked.

Her mother sighed and returned to her cooking. "You're a hard hearted woman sometimes."

"Or maybe I just respect myself more than you could ever understand. I could never live with a man who cheated on me. I expect fidelity as well as love."

"You'll get more reasonable once you marry. All women do."

Jillian shook her head. It was like her mother was speaking a language she didn't understand. "Mama, I have met the right man. I'm just having trouble believing in him. He keeps saying he loves me but I can't say it back. I go crawling into his bed to get what he's willing to give me, but I don't give him back what he wants in return. Why do you think that is?"

Her mother shrugged. "Probably because you're delusional about men and relationships. I blame this on your brother. If he'd lived, you'd have seen him change his tune too."

Jillian glared. "Jackson grew up to be an honorable man. God only knows what Daddy told him about women. Whatever it was, he was smart to set it aside. He made a great life with a great woman, Mama. His children are amazing. You and Daddy should be singing his praises instead of constantly harping about what you think he did wrong. My brother was a good man and a good person."

"Jackson's view of life was flawed. It's just a truth that we accept in this family. Your brother was weak. He could have done better for himself."

"You mean he could have married a woman he didn't love who he'd never be faithful to? Is that what you call better? Because I can tell you Jackson adored April. They worked each other the right way over and over to make those children and it shows in every one of them. Love and passion made those kids."

Her mother turned to glare at her. "Did you come here just to argue? I thought by now you would have forgiven me for making you mad."

"No, I didn't come to argue," Jillian said sharply. "I came to tell you that I'm pregnant. I just found out today."

"Oh, Jillian. How could you let that happen? I know you're

getting older but you're not married yet," her mother said sadly.

"That's just a legal detail. I'm keeping this child no matter what happens. I may even marry its father one day if he asks me. I have some things to work out first."

"Is it that professor at UK? He's not a great earner but he was quite handsome."

Jillian smirked. She didn't give a shit about money. She made her own damn money—good money. She was a self-made woman. "You don't know the father. He's a carpenter. I probably make twice what he does for a living."

"Oh, Jillian."

"Wait, there's more. He's white too," Jillian said flatly, now on a roll. "And he's the best man I've ever met. He treats me like a woman should be treated. You'll never get that but I don't care."

Her mother paled before her eyes. It was like she'd announced the father of her baby was the devil. Poor Jackson. Jillian wondered what her parents said to him when she hadn't been around. She also wondered why it had taken her so much longer in life to find the inner strength her brother had found when he was still just a kid.

And Zach was just like him. All of the kids were like him. Her brother had raised strong children and thank God for that. Damn, she missed him more than ever. He'd be proud of her today.

"This is all my fault," her mother said, sniffling. "This is my punishment for complaining about your father. You only did this to get back at him because you think he's broken my heart. That's simply not the case, Jillian. I was upset because he was in such a hurry to get back to her. And I told him he should have kept his mouth shut in front of you. Jackson found out the same way. Your father insinuates too much."

"So my brother knew about Dad cheating? That's how long it's been going on? No wonder Jackson turned his back on you all."

Her mother hung her head and sniffed at the tears rolling down her face. "I fussed at Jackson and he got that woman pregnant so she'd marry him. Now I've done the same thing to you. I need to learn to keep my mouth closed."

Jillian felt both numb and angry. It was a terrible combination.

"You had absolutely nothing to do with me getting pregnant. I thought my birth control was still working but it wasn't."

"And this is why you should have married years ago."

Jillian groaned. "Aren't you listening to anything? I never even looked twice at a man more light-skinned than me until this guy came along. You and daddy have talked about skin color so damn much that I incorporated those judgments into my own thinking without stopping to consider the problems I was bringing on myself. Luckily, what I feel for the father of my child is bigger than anything I've felt for a man before. We created a baby from a passion so pure and loving. I wish you could feel this just once with someone, Mama. You wouldn't care what color he was. Then you might actually understand both your son *and* your daughter."

Her mother eyes glazed over as she ignored everything Jillian said. But she was no longer surprised. Nor did she care when her mother started bemoaning having to share the news of the baby.

"This is going to kill your father. It's going to be like Jackson all over again. He got so mad at Jackson. I've never seen your father so mad. I wish you hadn't told me," her mother said sadly.

Jillian grunted with disgust. "I'm not worried about Daddy

getting mad. That's the only emotion I ever see him express anyway. He's never ever said he loves me—not once. You always say he does, but I've never heard it from him. All I hear is Daddy complaining about his golf shirts or the money he's spending. He is not a pleasant man. I don't know how you put up with him. I wouldn't. I think you should leave his cheating ass and teach him a lesson."

"Don't talk about your father that way. He deserves your respect."

"And I deserve his and yours because I have honored you both even when I didn't feel honored back," Jillian said firmly. She stared at her mother until the woman looked away. "At least I've seen what marriage is supposed to be like from friends. Maybe I won't screw up mine if I decide to go through with it. And Jackson set a fine example for me. God bless my brother's soul. Even if I don't get married, I've got a lot of decisions to make."

"You can't be thinking of raising your child alone, Jillian. Women with illegitimate children are seen as easy. Men come sniffing around and take advantage. Any husband is better than none. That's me to you as a woman even though I know your father will never feel that way."

Jillian shook her head. "You need counseling, Mama. God, I can only imagine what your childhood must have been like for you to think so black and white about everything under the sun. And I'm not talking skin color. I'm talking about all the messy, complicated, loving relationships that don't fit the box you think they should. What if I'd brought a black woman home and said I loved her? Would that have been better or worse for you and Daddy? I'd be interested to know what your bigotry is really about. I bet it has nothing to do with what you think it does."

"You would never have taken another woman to your bed. I raised you better," her mother said with confidence.

"Oh, please… it doesn't matter how you raised me. Love is messy and the world is full of gray. Or at least, my world is. Yours is too if you'd only open your eyes. You're living a lie."

"No, I'm living the life I want—the life I made for myself. Nobody's going to take it away from me either."

Jillian nodded. "Fair enough. I'm planning to do the same thing."

"Jillian, be sensible about this. How far along are you? There may be time for you to undo this madness. No one would know but us. I wouldn't tell a soul."

Jillian put a protective hand on her stomach. "Never talk about my child as anything but a blessing to me. I won't put up with it, especially not from you and your cheating husband. I can't even consider you two family anymore. You're both like strangers."

"Now you're really talking nonsense," her mother chastised.

"No, I'm talking about defending my child from people who want to harm him or her. Don't call me again until you're willing to welcome me and my family with open arms. And tell Daddy to keep his angry distance from me or I'll get a restraining order against him. Neither of you are getting a say in my life anymore. I'm done trying to love people who are never going to love me back."

"You can't mean such awful things. We raised you. We deserve better from you, Jillian."

"And children deserve to be loved by their parents without conditions. It's so clear to me now why my brother turned his back on you and Daddy. Wherever he and April are, I hope they're looking down and smiling on me for finally doing the right thing for myself. "

Jillian heard her mother weeping as she left but didn't even pause her stride. Her empathy was for one person only today. It was for the child growing inside her. At least that one priority was straight in her head.

Caring for Jackson's kids after he died had taught her what family was supposed to be. It was about the people who loved you whether they'd given birth to you or not. Shane and Reesa were doing a terrific job and adding to the family they taken into their hearts. Now she was getting her chance to bring her child into that same circle of love and caring.

She already knew what the Larson clan was going to say about the baby. Her child's acceptance was assured with them and that was no small matter in this divisive world.

Life was changing every moment, but she was going to be alright with that. The process of freeing her mind from her past might not go smoothly, but it would happen. Her child and its Celtic smart-ass father would probably both see to that.

Every revolution required some sacrifice—internal or external. She felt like she'd just made her biggest one in giving up a life plan that hadn't made room for changing her mind or the gift she now carried inside.

It also hadn't made room for a man who made her feel the way Joe always did.

Her mind was finally clear about him too. She knew what was important to her now and the list was short.

Man. Child. Love.

It was time to stop planning and begin living.

"Nursing is fine and I'm producing okay, but Jude eats so much I'm having to supplement with formula. On the plus side though, I plan those feedings around the nanny Shane hired who comes by to help. I nap while Abigail takes care of him. Bottle feeding is wonderful."

"That's great," Jillian said, finishing the diaper. She looked at Jude's tiny mama watching her every move. "How do you hold him? The boy's half the size you are already."

"Oh, he's not that big," Reesa said with a frown. "You're exaggerating."

"How big do you think he's going to be in a month or two?"

Reesa picked up her son and held him close. "I imagine he'll be a bit bigger than most children. Ellen said Shane were always bigger. She said that she and Will taught Shane to be really gentle so he wouldn't hurt the other kids."

Jillian laughed. "Is your big old Viking gentle?"

Reesa's mouth quirked. "When he needs to be. Sometimes I like it when he's not."

"Girlfriend, that evidence speaks for itself. Give me my

nephew," Jillian demanded as she stole the baby from Reesa's arms and carried him to the living room.

She sat in the biggest of the two rockers there and studied his contented face. The baby ate and slept, contentedly unaware of any drama going on around him. How wonderful would that be?

"Even swaddling your son is a challenge. Where did you get these oversized blankets?"

"Ellen had them made months ago. She said she had a feeling the baby would need them."

Laughing, Jillian smiled at the baby in her arms. "Jude, you sure picked a crazy family to be born into. Better brace yourself. Your name is Larson."

Reesa grabbed her postpartum pillow and pressed it to her abdomen as she sat in the smaller-sized rocker that Shane had insisted they buy. "You're looking happier. I'm glad. I've been worried about you."

"Maybe I'm relieved you survived the baby's birth without any problems," Jillian said, not looking at her friend.

"That's not it," Reesa said, studying Jillian. "You're… glowing. Did you fall in love with your booty call guy?"

Jillian laughed. "Something like that."

"Something like that?" Reesa asked with a smile.

"Remember when you said our children might get to grow up together if I got busy?"

Reesa jumped up and squealed, pressing the pillow to her stomach when it hurt. "Damn. I forget I can't do that yet. *Jillian, are you pregnant?*"

"Knocked up big time," Jillian confirmed, laughing at Reesa's happy groaning. "I don't know much yet so don't ask me a bunch of questions. My first baby appointment is next week."

"That's so wonderful. I hope you're happy." Reesa came over and hugged her hard.

"I'm happier than I ever imagined being, but you can't say anything. I haven't told the father yet. I'm being a big old chicken about it."

"Why? Joe's going to be thrilled. He'll probably use it as leverage to get you to marry him," Reesa said, hugging harder. "I'm so glad you worked things out."

"How do you…" Surprised Jillian squeezed Jude too tightly and he grunted loudly at the uncomfortable pressure. "Your son says stop hugging me. He can't sleep."

Reesa chuckled as she hobbled back to her rocker. "I saw the way Joe looked at you. I knew it was just a matter of time. I know Joe doesn't fit your great plan…"

"Screw the plan. I trash canned the plan for good today," Jillian said. "I found out my father has been openly cheating on my mother for years. I don't think they ever loved each other. That's the kind of family I came from. Apparently my brother knew about it before he died—maybe even before he married April."

Reesa squirmed in her seat. "It was after they married. April was so shocked that she told me some of things Jackson told her about finding out. She said he planned on telling you when you got older. You and I were still in college at the time. I know your brother definitely didn't want you to find out like he did."

"Mama told me Daddy said something in front of him."

"Maybe, but April said Jackson caught him with someone at an away game. Your father came to all of them, but never alone. Jackson stopped buying the friend story when he saw your father kissing a woman on the lips. Your father refused to discuss it with him. Jackson never had much to do with your after that time."

"Poor Jackson. I wish he'd just told me back then," Jillian

said. She tilted her head. "If you knew all this time, why didn't you tell me?"

"It was second-hand information from my sister and Jackson wanted to tell you himself. After Jackson and April died, I forgot about it. I was too busy trying to come up with money to fight your parents for custody in court. How did it come up in conversation for you?"

"Mama slipped up when she was fighting with Daddy about golf shirts. He was planning a trip to Florida to spend two weeks with his latest fling. She complained about the woman. She admitted there had been a lot of them over the years. She has a solid prenup that my grandmother had her draw up before they married which is the only reason I think Daddy keeps coming back."

"How much does finding out all that stuff about them bother you?"

"You know I don't like cheaters, but that's their business. What bothers me is all those years I based my hunt for the perfect man on their criteria. I was damaged by their opinions and by wanting love and acceptance. But how can they give me unconditional love when they don't even care about each other? The bottom line is that they can't. Even as old as I am, that was hard to accept."

"I'm sorry. If you'd ever mentioned any doubts, I would have told you what I knew."

"I know you would have," Jillian grumbled. "Guess it wasn't my destiny to know until now."

"That sounds like something Joe would say."

Jillian snorted. "Seriously—did Shane say anything about me and Joe?"

"Shane doesn't know anything except that Joe likes you. Shane would have told me if he suspected you were getting together."

"We haven't even been out in public yet. I just keep showing up at his house. Does that count as together?"

Reesa laughed. "Shane kept showing up at my house and now I'm recovering from a C-section."

"Well, that's because you had to have that big old Viking. Don't complain to me. I tried to find you someone closer to your own size."

Giggling, Reesa moaned. "Well, he's getting snipped soon so this can't happen again. That's going to be great."

"Snipped?"

Reese nodded. "I'm thirty-five and done. Five children is enough motherhood for me. Shane agrees. He's happy to have his son and thanks me daily. How many are you planning to have? You're going to have to keep busy to squeeze in one more before you're forty."

"Stop scaring me," Jillian ordered, squeezing Jude too tightly again. His mother laughed at her. "I can only handle thinking about creating one red-haired monster at a time. The father may not want this one."

"Shane said Joe hasn't gone out bar-hopping since our wedding. He stays home and watches TV, though Shane did say he'd found a hobby recently. Shane said he thought Joe had fallen in love. Was he right?"

Jillian sighed. Apparently her secret man wasn't so secret after all. "That's what he tells me."

"Don't you believe him? Joe comes off like a horn-dog but he's actually a really good guy. Shane lectures him all the time for all the work he does for free."

"Joseph is a great guy," Jillian said. "I'm just..." She glared at her friend. "I don't remember you rushing to commit."

Reesa laughed. "Can you say bossy Larson male without laughing at Shane tricking me into marrying him? I know Joe is not like that. No one is like that. Shane's lucky I loved him back."

Jillian did laugh. "No, Joe's not like that. But he's not a saint either."

"Who would want a saint?" Reesa demanded with a grin. "Sex would be awful with someone who hadn't practiced. A little bit of training is fine but a virgin? No, thank you. The guy needs to at least know where all the buttons and slots are."

Giggling, Jillian picked up Jude and held him in front of her. "Are you hearing your Mama?"

"My son's a Larson…" Reesa said with a giggle.

"Right. What was I thinking? Go back to sleep. You're too young to hear this shit," Jillian said, snuggling Jude back into her arms while his mother laughed.

"Are you going to Carrie's African art show tonight?"

"I didn't know there was one," Jillian said.

"Some mystery artist she found." Reesa fetched one of the tickets Shane had solicited from Carrie. "Here. I'm not going obviously. Shane isn't either. Do you want more than one? We have extras."

Jillian thought about it as she passed Jude to Reesa. She and Joe hadn't even been out in public together. An African art show might not be the best first date for that. "Just give me one ticket. I don't know if I'll go or not and there's no need to waste them. Chelsea and Brian should go. Zach too if he can."

"Will's coming to get the kids. You should go," Reesa said.

"Why?"

Reesa sat down carefully doing her best not to wake her son. "Maybe the art will provide some clarity. Your heritage will always be your heritage. It will be your child's heritage too. I'd say invite Joe, but I don't want to be pushy."

"I should," Jillian said and sent a text before she changed her mind. She frowned at the display when he finally answered. "He said he'd love to go and would see me there. He said he finished Carrie's walls today. I have no idea what that means."

Reesa laughed. "He built portable walls for the gallery. Carrie probably gave him a ticket."

"Oh. Now that makes some sense. Why would she give him a ticket to an African art showing?"

Reesa gave her a look. "Did you just say *you people*? I know you did not."

Jillian laughed. "You're right. I did. Damn it. He'll probably enjoy it. Do you know what his hobby is now? Did Shane tell you?"

Reesa shook her head.

Jillian smiled. "Will gave him carving lessons. He made a damn good rhino out of wood. I hope he makes a lot more." She stopped and then laughed. "He hides his hobby in a second bedroom that he keeps locked. Do you think there's any way…?"

"Joe?" Reesa said, shaking her head. "I don't think so. Shane would never have been able to keep that kind of thing to himself. None of the Larsons would. They see Joe as one of them. They'd be shouting it to the world."

"Yeah. You're right," Jillian said.

But her mind went back to how good that little rhino had been. She'd bet money that it was as good as anything Carrie had on display.

AT FOUR THAT AFTERNOON, JOE ROLLED THE LAST WALL INTO PLACE
while trying his best not to watch Carrie moving pieces of his
art work around. There were polished counters of vignettes and
pedestals for some of the bigger pieces. Somehow she'd spread
them everywhere. His work seemed to be the only art visible in
the gallery.

Seeing it tied his stomach into knots. "I need to leave before
I throw up on your floor," Joe said.

Carrie laughed and kept on moving. "Nervous about
tonight?"

"No. I'm terrified," Joe corrected. He pointed at a counter.
"Why do some of the pieces have different colored tags?"

"Some are sold already," Carrie said, turning quickly away
before she revealed too much.

"Sold?" Joe said in surprise walking over to one. He glanced
at the tag. "Sold to who?"

"Remember I told you that several galleries had put
deposits against getting to pick out pieces they wanted?"

"Yes," Joe answered.

Carrie lifted a shoulder. "I've sold a third of your work already. Word is getting out. I told you this kind of art was hard to find."

"But…" Joe looked around. He wandered from pedestal to pedestal and counter-to-counter. He could see no logic in what was marked as already sold. "I'm shocked."

"Me too," Carrie said. "Before I even sold the first piece, I'd doubled the original prices I showed you. I did that after bargaining with the first gallery over the two pieces they wanted. Tomorrow we'll mark up the remaining ones further that don't sell this evening. I don't want to give your art away but I don't have time to change price tags again before the showing. I could have probably gotten a bit more for all of them, but getting a quantity sold is the end result."

"Carrie…"

She turned to Joe and smiled. "I know I'm pretty distracted right now. We can talk tomorrow and I'll lay it all out for you. Do you need another installment against your earnings? I can write you a check for another ten thousand right now."

"Why would I need more? I haven't cashed the last check you gave me. What am I supposed to do with the money?"

Carrie stopped and sighed. "Spend it. Use it. Buy exotic wood and keep carving. By the way, I put my name on two pieces which I'm purchasing for the gallery's permanent collection. You'll have to tell me later where you got that wood. You definitely need to make more things in it."

"My supplier is my biggest secret," Joe joked, trying to gauge her seriousness as she hustled toward her office. Any second now he expected Carrie to turn around and yell "Psyche!" before demanding her money back.

"Why are you still here?" Carrie yelled from across the floor. "Go put on that new suit and come back fashionably late. Have a few drinks and call for an Uber ride. I think you might need it. And find your balls before you come back, Joseph. Artists are supposed to be arrogant not humble. Humility does not sell as well."

Joe stood in the middle of what his obsession with Jillian had spawned and wondered why he'd ever thought selling his work would be a good idea. He wondered how long it would take him to shove it all into a bag and make a run for it.

Carrie came out of her office and marched over to him. "I see that look in your eyes. We're under contract, buddy. There's no backing out now." She pressed a piece of paper into his hand. "Here's your check."

"I told you I didn't need…"

"For the walls, Joe."

"Oh," he said, unfolding the paper in his hand. The small number made him laugh. "I'm a mess, aren't I?"

"There's always a first showing and it's always like this. I've showcased a lot of first-timers. It's both thrilling and scary. Did you set up the big piece?"

Joe nodded. "It's on the rolling pedestal and I put the velvet drape over it like you said."

"Excellent. That's going to be my surprise as well. I'm going to roll it out mid-way through the evening and do a big reveal. If you're feeling brave, you can join me for that. If not, I'll do the honors alone. Whatever you decide is fine with me."

"I don't know," Joe said.

When that piece was unveiled, everyone was going to know the biggest secret Joe was keeping. And it wasn't that he was making African art.

Joe blew out a breath. He could probably get by with sneaking the big piece back out of here. No one had seen it yet —not even Carrie. But what would one piece matter?

"I may not come back if I leave," Joe warned.

Carrie shrugged and tugged on his arm. She walked him to

the back door of the gallery where she knew his truck was parked in her unloading zone.

"If you don't show back up, I will see you tomorrow morning. I have to go get dressed and kiss my daughter before she falls asleep without seeing me. I'll be back here within the hour. Doors open at seven. There was so much local interest that I had to issue tickets and I had to stop issuing them before reaching the fire limit. We may have to do a second show for the people who didn't get in tonight. Shane took several tickets and I sent two to Simba. He might recognize your work, but I warned him the artist wasn't ready to announce his identity. Hopefully, he takes a hint."

Joe thought he might as well have taken out a front page ad in the Lexington Herald-Leader. Carrie had contacted newspapers and the local TV stations. What was going to happen if he didn't show back up?

Head spinning, Joe climbed into his truck and drove home on autopilot. He didn't even remember making the trip. Pulling out the hundred dollar bottle of whiskey he'd splurged on at Christmas, he downed two shots before heading to put on his new monkey clothes.

God help him if this had been the wrong way to prove to Jillian how he felt.

JILLIAN HANDED OVER HER TICKET TO BRANDON BARRYMORE WHO was on door duty tonight. "Hi Jillian. Thanks for coming to our showing of African Dreams. Hope you enjoy the evening. Do you know if Chelsea is coming?"

"I think Will is bringing her."

"Awesome... I mean, great. She shouldn't miss this. Carrie

says the artist is someone local, but it's all a big secret," Brandon said, his face lighting with joy.

"We all got those, don't we?" Jillian told him with a wink, charmed when the boy blushed at her teasing.

Love was for the young, she thought. They knew how to give themselves fully to it.

Jillian hugged the boy before heading inside. She walked until she reached the main floor. The smell of wood hit her. It was familiar and soothing. It made her feel safe and at home. What a strange thing to be feeling…

"Wow—that dress shows off everything just right," Joe said in her ear.

He handed her a glass a wine. "Pinot Noir."

"I'm only going to be able to have a couple sips…" Jillian stopped, appalled at what she'd almost said to him.

"I hear you," Joe said. "Wine is fun, but I'm not sure the hangover was worth it."

"Uh…" Jillian said, then took a big gulp to cool her heated face. "Joe, I…"

"What do you think?" Joe said, pointing to the art around them.

Jillian turned and scanned the pieces. "They're wonderful, but I think your rhino could carry his own here. I'm no art critic like Carrie but I think your work is just as good as this artist's."

Laughing, Joe ran a hand over his hair. "Thank you. You have no idea what that means to me."

"Don't do that," Jillian said, and pulled his hand down. "Hair like yours doesn't fall back into place on its own. Messed up hair is not going to match that great suit you're wearing."

"Joe?" Simba said, stopping by them. "Good to see you again. You've been busy."

Simba's date was hugging Jillian and complimenting her

dress. Joe looked on and smiled while he hoped no one heard Simba talking to him.

"It's all in your head, you know. All those concerns," Simba whispered softly. "Art is a bridge. Walk across it, Joseph. You don't have stay a carpenter forever. You can stop right after you build my bookcases."

"I promise you're next on my list," Joe promised.

"Never doubted it," Simba said with a smile and put a hand on his date's arm. "Let's get some wine before Joe drinks it all. He seems nervous tonight. Never trust an Irishman around free booze."

Joe laughed and put a trembling hand in his pocket. Nervous didn't even begin to describe what he was feeling. He turned to Jillian. "Did you bring a date?"

"Sort of. He said he'd meet me here."

"Bastard. He should have at least offered to pick you up." Joe grinned at her chuckle. "Want to look around?"

Jillian nodded and started forward. She paused at counters and pedestals. They were all very good. She pointed to a woman. "Do you think that looks like me?"

"Give me a moment." Joe glanced at the statue and closed his eyes. "I'm trying to imagine you in an African wrap dress."

Her hand pushing on his arm had his eyes popping open. She moved on to the next set of pieces. Joe tried not to notice Carrie and Drake discreetly moving among the pieces and changing the tags to ones marking them as sold.

Jillian sighed. "He's very good. Do you think this is his first showing? I don't understand why he's keeping it such a big secret."

Joe nodded. "I do."

"Oh, look, Joseph," Jillian said in excitement. "Your rhino would look perfect next to that lion. See I told you that your work was just as good."

"They were carved at about the same time." Joe slipped his hand into his coat pocket and pulled out the rhino. He set it next to the lion. "I sort of thought of them as a set, but in the end, I gave him up."

Jillian picked up the rhino and held it in her hand. "Are you saying…?"

People nearby stopped to listen to him and Jillian… and to watch as the rhino got hugged to Jillian's beautiful breasts.

"Come on," Joe whispered. "I have something better to show you. Remember you asked me to make you a piece? Well, I sort of did."

Joe waved to Carrie who nodded to someone across the room. Brandon rolled out a pedestal covered in velvet. Joe let go of Jillian's hand and stepped to the side of it. "This piece is called The Color of Love. What do you think?"

Joe slid the cloth from the bust he'd carved and whispers filtered through the crowed.

Jillian stepped forward and looked up into her own face. She ran her painted fingertips across her cheeks before dropping them to skim across the statue's growing belly. Only a sheer cloth covered her swollen breasts. This was how Joe saw her. There were no secrets left.

"Did your Celtic ancestors make you psychic? How do you always know?" Jillian asked.

"Know what?" Joe asked. "How do I know I love you? How do I know that you are the woman I've been looking for all my life? I think what pushed me over the edge was getting hit with a pillow over and over for no good reason. It was the first time I was ever attracted by an act of female insanity."

The crowd tittered but all Joe heard was Jillian chuckling at his teasing. He wanted to make her laugh for the rest of their lives.

"Joseph McEldowney," Jillian said loudly, pitching her voice above the crowd.

"Yes, Jillian Lansing," Joe answered loudly back.

"I love you, Joseph. Will you marry me and make me that way? I don't want that to just be a statue of me. I want that to be me," she said, pointing to the statue's protruding stomach.

She'd tell him about the baby later—but in private. They were already giving people enough gossip to chew on.

In the silence that descended after Jillian's proposal, Joe heard nothing but the blood rushing in his ears. "Are you sure about this? Are you clear?"

"Yes, Joe. I'm finally sure and I'm finally clear. I'm sorry it took me so long."

Joe didn't see anything but her as he pulled Jillian into his arms. "Thank God. Yes. My answer is yes. Please don't change your mind. I'm all out of wood."

Jillian laughed as she hugged her husband to be. He was nothing she'd planned and everything she'd been searching for.

Tonight in her prayers she'd thank her ancestors for all they'd done in getting her into his arms.

EPILOGUE

The smell of wood didn't greet her when she came through the door. She missed that a little, but it meant Joe had finally moved the torso of her into what he called *the study* and what she called *the library*. Whichever name it went by, it was one of their favorite rooms. It contained a giant stone fireplace with a gas insert and wall-to-wall bookcases. They'd bought a giant desk for the room that no one used but just because they both liked seeing it there.

God help her, Joe's old couch was front and center and faced the fireplace. It needed to be put out of its misery, but would have to do until she could find the furniture she wanted. It had made Joe happy not to throw it away. Maybe she'd see about having it rebuilt and reupholstered. That would make her frugal husband happy. Who knew what would happened when her nesting urges started kicking in? She sure didn't. Along with rugs and towels, Reesa had replaced every pillow and blanket in her whole house before Jude was born. The kids still laughed about their aunt changing out everything that wasn't furniture.

The library—and they were going to be calling it that if she got her way—also held some of Joe's art. Today African queen —her name for the statue—had joined the other work because she hadn't been able to get used to seeing her own face every time she walked in her front door.

The Color Of Love had once been Joe's showpiece but he'd done two more torsos on commission since the original gallery showing. Her husband had been offered a lot of money for the elongated bust, but had absolutely refused to let it go. As a compromise, Carrie was offering to rent it to galleries for shows featuring other pieces of Joe's work. He had said the money from those rentals would technically be hers since the piece was hers. Jillian was already seeing a healthy college fund growing.

"Joe?" she called, hanging up her purse and keys on the antique coat rack bench combo that Will and Jessica had given them when they bought the house. It was a beautiful piece of furniture that looked right at home in her foyer.

"I'm in the kitchen," Joe yelled back.

The partially restored Victorian they'd bought was magnificent, and best of all had some already renovated rooms downstairs, including a first floor master suite to die for and a gourmet kitchen. Some local architect had started the work on it and moved before finishing. Buying a house with their living quarters in pristine condition had mattered most to her. What mattered most to Joe was that pizza place now had no trouble filling their order.

The upstairs was still a work in progress but Joe promised to get to some of it before the baby came. Chelsea was going to live with them for her first semester of college to help with the baby.

Life had moved quickly in the last two months, but Jillian had no regrets. How could she when every day just kept getting better and better? Neither Joe's father or her parents had attended their wedding. They had sent invitations which had been ignored. Ellen had happily arranged it all in two weeks and everything had been incredibly beautiful. Ellen declared it her first true success because for once nobody fainted, got drunk, or embarrassed the minister.

Jillian smiled as she entered the welcoming room and saw her husband leaning against the granite top of their big island. This room was incredible. She was going to have to learn to use it. Maybe she'd take lessons while she was off on maternity leave.

"Something smells really good in here."

"Why are you always surprised? I told you I could cook," he teased.

"Uh huh…" Jillian said with a grin, snatching a kiss before she peered into the oven. "Reesa walk you through another recipe over the phone?"

Joe chuckled. "No, she brought by a casserole this time and left me a written version of how to make it. I worked late and didn't feel like takeout. I need lessons if I'm going to be the chef around here."

"I'll handle dish duty. I don't mind loading the dishwasher." Jillian laughed as she pulled her husband's hands around her waist to make him hold her. Joe always chuckled when she did that and hugged her tight enough to steal her breath.

"I see you moved the statue today."

"Did you also noticed that I put your giant fishbowl of flowers on the table instead? Now I have to worry about some Larson kid knocking it over on themselves. Though not unexpected, Ivy is a little terror when she visits. "

"I think she's a sweetie. She kisses my belly and talks about the *bebee*. Little girlfriend going to be up to her ears in *bebees* shortly." Jillian confessed as she laughed. "All children are like that at her age."

"Then your fancy fishbowl for flowers has to go."

"I did miss the instant smell of wood when I came in. Maybe you can make something else for the foyer."

"How about a big wooden bowl? You can fill it with lightweight things that won't cause concussions."

Jillian thought about it and nodded. "Would you make it from ebony wood? I'd love that."

"Sure," Joe said. "I've got a new delivery arriving soon. I asked for some bigger chunks this time."

Joe's phone buzzed against the granite. He picked it up and grinned. "Brooke's in final stages of labor but Shane says the baby hasn't crowned yet. It scares the shit out of me that I actually know what that means."

"How long has labor been going on?"

"It's been at least six hours. They gave her that stuff they gave Reesa though. I heard she's been singing. I wish one of the nurses had taken a photo of Drake's face."

Jillian winced as she laughed. "Poor woman. I might just schedule a C-section whether I need it or not. At least it's over quickly."

"Let's eat then we'll pop over to the hospital and check on Drake. He could probably use some normal people to talk to. Michael and Shane have been there the whole time. Will has his hands full because Jessica had to take something to stop her meltdown over Brooke being in labor. And Brandon's still at work. Every time Drake comes out of the room, those are the people he sees. The man needs us."

Jillian chuckled. She was working through it. She was getting there. But her true thoughts popped out anyway. *"Normal people?* When did the interracial couple in this group become classified as the normal people?"

Joe laughed. "I guess that did seem a little ironic when I said it, but you have to admit most people would look normal next to the Larson men."

"True," Jillian said, toying with Joe's shirt. "Are you happy with us, Mr. McEldowney?"

Joe lifted a hand to her cheek. "Happier than I ever dreamed of being, Mrs. McEldowney."

Jillian exaggerated her sigh. "Well, okay then. Let's go play normal people and help bring another *bebee* into the world."

"Then maybe we can come home and make one of our own," Joe said hopefully.

Jillian drew back and pointed downward as she gave him the stink eye. "Don't you think we better wait until this one gets done cooking before we make another one?"

"Oh, yeah," Joe said, chuckling at her mock-glare. "You look so hot in that dress that my libido momentarily forgot it had already put a bun in your oven."

"And this is what I married…" Jillian said, backing away. "I'm going to go change into something less hot."

"Good luck finding that in your closet," Joe said. "I love you. Hurry back and we'll eat."

"I love you too, Joseph."

"Need some help changing?" Joe asked.

"Oh, hell no," Jillian said, hustling to get away. "You stay right here. I know how you are."

"Me? I know how *we* are," Joe corrected.

"We are fine," Jillian said with determination. "But we have things to do. My husband says we have to go be normal. I hope I have something normal in my closet. I don't even know what normal people wear. This is not going to be easy. See you in an hour or two."

Happier with his life than he'd ever dreamed of being, Joe laughed at the sassy wife he adored. He grinned as he wondered how many *bebees* Jillian was going to be willing to make with him. He couldn't wait to find out.

– THE END –

NOTE FROM THE AUTHOR

Thank you for reading *Carved In Wood*!

If you enjoyed reading this book, please consider leaving a positive review or rating on the site where you purchased it. Reader reviews help my books continue to be valued by distributors/resellers and help new readers make decisions about reading them.

You are the reason I write these stories and I sincerely appreciate you!

Many thanks for your support,
~ Donna McDonald

www.donnamcdonaldauthor.com

Join my mailing list to hear about new releases.

WHAT'S COMING NEXT IN AOL?

This is always the question.

The answer is that I don't know. I don't have anything planned for the *Art Of Love* series in the near future, but I might double-back and write about Brandon and Chelsea sometime. I never say never anymore. I don't like saying goodbye to my characters anymore than readers do.

In the back of this book I have included a long excerpt from Book 1 of my latest contemporary series. The language and sex are dialed back a little, but the sensuality has been cranked up to compensate for closing the door.

All the humor you're used to is still there in *The Perfect Date* series, as well as new heroes and heroines to love. Seven books in that series are already published. Hope you give my other work a try.

Happy reading,
xoxo Donna

EXCERPT: NEVER IS A VERY LONG TIME

THE PERFECT DATE SERIES, BOOK 1

BOOK DESCRIPTION

Cupid she's not—but she's pretty darn close.

Nothing in the world feels better than finding her clients the perfect date. Of course finding one for herself might be nice, but creative bill paying is for college students—not for accomplished doctors in their forties. Satisfied customers keep the electricity on.

But wait, according to all the magazines the forties are the new twenties. Now if only she felt twenty…

Everything in Dr. Mariah Bates' life was perfectly fine until the moment she quit her celebrity radio job to start a dating business. Two years, a cheating ex, and a very ugly divorce later, she's suddenly homeless and living with her mother. Not exactly how she'd envisioned her life working out. Not that her mom isn't great, but come on.

With her cop ex-husband doing everything he can to ruin her

business, she's at her wit's end. Throw in another cop who makes her believe in love at first sight—or at least lust—and life is a mess. Interesting, fun and tummy tingling, but a mess. Especially since another cop is the last thing she needs.

Despite a very persistent, want-to-be beau who insists he's protecting her, it's time for Mariah to take control of the game her ex has been playing. Punt or pass, she's due for a touchdown.

Everyone deserves the perfect date—even her.

1

MARIAH FLINCHED AS THE WOODEN GAVEL HIT THE BLOCK IN FRONT of the judge.

"I'll hear from the defendant's attorney now."

Beside her, Bill rose and nodded once to recognize the judge's request.

"Your Honor—not to denigrate the fine work done by most detectives in our local police precincts, but the charges brought by my client's ex-husband, Detective Luray, are not backed by anything of substance. Dating services are a dime a dozen these days... no offense to my own client... but I'm having a hard time figuring out the grounds for the illegal solicitation charge the Prosecuting Attorney's office is attempting to press."

Mariah saw the judge look past her attorney to her. She was frowning and all but glaring. Dan wanted her to suffer for divorcing him and it looked as if he was actually going to get his way.

"Thank you, Counselor. Now I believe I'd like to hear your client's own defense of the charges against her," the judge declared.

"Yes, Your Honor." Bill leaned in. "Tell her your story, Mariah."

Mariah stood. "Your Honor, my name is Dr. Mariah Bates. I have a PhD in Psychology from Johns Hopkins. I am a licensed and certified marriage and relationship therapist. For over twenty years, I did a call-in radio show that helped people with their relationship issues. Now my primary business is an elite, professional dating service that is really more like a matchmaking service for busy professionals. We're a bit like Kellerher International, which is widely known, and as far as I know, quite well respected."

"If I might interject..." the prosecutor said loudly. "Dr. Bates's business does not offer access to a dating database of potential matches nor does she offer anyone a phone app as do most services of her kind. Nothing discovered in her business model indicates she is offering any ongoing match service, but rather she is selling individual time spent with a client to yet another client. It is reasonable to conclude that her business model is a potential cover for nefarious escort activities."

Mariah felt her jaw tighten. There had been no discovery at all. No one had subpoenaed her records. No, Dan had given the Hamilton County prosecutor all that misinformation. But who was going to doubt one of Cincinnati's finest?

"We charge a flat fee per service which translates in most cases to a flat fee per date. The person we find the match for pays the fee, especially if there is a pressing need, such as a business function, wedding, or other social gathering where the client feels it would be best to have a companion at his or her side. We are not following the subscription model because of discretion. This is the same reason we don't use anything like an app. Our clients are CEOs, local celebrities, sports figures, and have other high profile jobs. We work to protect the privacy of every client we help."

She turned her head to the man seated several rows behind her wearing a very expensive suit she'd bought for him five years ago. It was easier today to ignore how good Dan looked in it. Her bitterness over his actions had torn away the rose colored glasses she normally viewed him through.

"As I have repeatedly told my ex-husband, Detective Daniel Luray, the way I bill is not proof of solicitation. Instead, it provides me a reasonable cash flow to continue serving my clients. Fostering twenty-two weddings among clients last year could be used as proof of my matchmaking success, if such proof is necessary. My clients are business people who would not appreciate their carefully selected date being called an "escort" for no good reason other than Detective Luray's unfounded suspicions or his desire to get back at me for having had the nerve to divorce him."

The judge looked at the prosecutor. "Is there any real evidence against Dr. Bates's company? Any client claiming they paid for sex and didn't get any? Anybody saying they're being pimped out by Dr. Bates?"

"Not yet, Your Honor, but…"

She didn't allow the prosecutor to waffle any further. The judge's gavel hit her wooden block. "Case dismissed due to lack of evidence. Dr. Bates, we are sorry to have wasted your time this morning."

"Thank you, Your Honor," Mariah said, breathing out at last.

Bill reached over and hugged her. "You could have mentioned me and Abby, you know. We're proof of your success and you didn't even have the agency then."

Mariah shook her head. "Dan's vendetta against me is no reason to drag my friends down into the mud. It's bad enough he has me wrestling around with him in it."

She gathered up her things and moved to walk out. Bill

walked closely behind. She should have guessed it wasn't going to be that easy.

"One day I will get what I need for evidence, Mariah. I'm going to be watching your ass very closely," Dan warned as she walked by him.

"Great news. Kiss my ass while you're back there nosing around," Mariah ordered, striding away from the man she had loved forever but now loathed.

Behind her, she heard Bill say something to Dan, but it was probably best she not know what passed between the two men. All of her friends had taken her side in the divorce when her long time, nice husband had suddenly turned into an ass just because she quit a lucrative job to start a more risky one. Their loyalty to her had gotten even stronger after the divorce was final and Dan was seen around town with some yet to be named bleached-hair blonde on his arm.

Mariah huffed because crying over the sad state of her love life was out of the question. She was beyond emotional hurt now. That kind of hurt had come when she went off the air and decided to do something different because she needed to feel alive and not just on autopilot. The emotional hurt had come with the thousand arguments she and Dan had frequently had about their financial inequities and her earning power—the net result being a property settlement that left her literally homeless. Dan had come out of the divorce as well as any greedy, manipulating spouse ever could have. She'd come out of it stripped of half her wealth, but missing most of her dignity.

But the good news for Mariah was that the legal cords were finally all cut. That was what mattered to her these days. Now she could move forward the way she needed to. She'd been like a rabid, trapped wolf at the end of her divorce proceedings. She'd been willing to sacrifice an arm, a leg, and the nearly million dollar home she and Dan had bought with her celebrity earnings.

Setting the trumped up criminal charges she'd just faced aside, Mariah actually thought she *had* escaped. Unfortunately, Dan continued to be there on the edges of her life—still poking and prodding at a decision he thought he had some right to have an opinion about.

Why did he bother with trying to hurt her? She'd already given him the lion's share of their possessions. Her mind kept churning on the issue, but the truth was unknowable. When your once loving husband became greedy and spiteful, there was no more pretending you understood him.

When it came right down to it, there was only one thing Mariah knew for certain these days. Divorcing Dan had put her off all men for a good long while. She could only hope her own sad relationship story wasn't going to be bad for her matchmaking business.

2

"Mariah?"

Mariah lifted her head from her laptop and the task she'd hoped would distract her from her woes. Dr. Della Livingston, her twenty-seven year old multi-tasking miracle who worked mostly in exchange for research data for her book, looked ready to have a meltdown. "What's wrong, Della?"

"I know you just got back from court, but there's a Detective Monroe here asking to see you. He says he was referred by someone."

"Oh, for pity's sake. I've had enough of this," Mariah said, rising from her chair.

She straightened her unfortunately super snug pencil skirt back down over her hips. Both pieces of her favorite suit had gotten tighter in the last couple of years, but it was still the best one she owned. That was why she'd chosen it to wear to court. The light shade of rose flattered her blonde complexion without looking too feminine.

Mariah marched to the door of her office. Taking one more deep breath, she moved by a still cringing Della, until she was standing in front of the still seated man. She glared down at him. "What can I do for you, Detective Monroe?"

To her annoyance, the man's face blushed crimson just at hearing her tone. His gray eyes briefly dropped down to her legs, but they didn't linger there long, before returning to her face. Good thing too. With that much gray at his temples, the man damn well ought to know better.

"Is that how you typically greet your prospective clients?" he managed to choke out.

"No," Mariah declared flatly. "It's how I greet sleazy cop buddies of my detective ex-husband who think they're going to come around and dig into my business for no good reason. The charges were dismissed today due to lack of evidence. You've got a lot of damn nerve showing up here."

"Uh… that's not why I came," he stammered out. Then his brow furrowed. "Who's your detective ex?"

"Don't waste my time with inane questions," Mariah ordered. She watched him reach up and run a nervous hand thorough his perfectly cut hair. Had the man really believed she'd accept his lame story? It would be just like Dan to plant someone as a client here to spy for him. Well, she was not buying this new detective's innocent act.

The man cleared his throat and stood, towering above her by a good foot or more even in her heels. Her gaze traveled up to his now pained-filled gray eyes. She glared until he finally looked away from her.

"I believe I made a mistake in coming here. Elliston said you were… well, it doesn't matter. Sorry to have bothered you."

"Elliston?"

"McElroy," he said tightly. "Geeky nephew of mine. Said you were fixing him up with the perfect woman."

Hands that had been fisted on her hips dropped to her side. "I will neither confirm nor deny to you that anyone is or is not a client of my business. Privacy is not just a buzz word I throw around. However, I appreciate all referrals. If this was an honest one, I'm sorry for jumping to wrong conclusions."

He studied her for a few long moments and Mariah let him get by with it. The silence helped to calm her.

"Bad day?" he asked.

Mariah nodded. Why not confess? If the man was lying to her, Dan had already told him anyway. "Nothing life changing, but I had to go to court this morning. The experience left me a little less trusting of anyone with the first name of *Detective*."

"I caught the gist of that in your greeting. Ex causing you problems?"

"Let's just say I'm not at my best at the moment, so this unfruitful conversation can end."

His almost bashful smile over her defensiveness did strange things to her insides. What she felt in the lower regions of her body made her mad at herself. However, if he truly was Elliston McElroy's uncle, she needed to be polite.

"Let's start again." Mariah put out her hand to shake. "I'm Dr. Mariah Bates—the owner, CEO, and general doer of every role here at *The Perfect Date*."

He stared at her hand for a split second longer than proper, then swallowed her hand with his own extremely large one. He didn't shake it so much as hold it for a moment. Mariah had to stop herself from wiping her hand on her skirt when he let go. "What can I do for you, Detective?"

"First name's actually John—not Detective," he said, correcting her. "And I'm thinking coming here really wasn't the best idea. Can we just pretend I wasn't here at all?"

Mariah rolled her eyes and drew in a breath. "Look, Detective Monroe…"

"John…" he corrected again.

Mariah sighed. "Look… *John*… normally I'd sit out here and

talk you into feeling a certain comfort level before coaxing you into my office for a more private chat. Seeing as how I've already yelled at you and accused you of many things you profess to be innocent of…"

"Well, I…"

Mariah held a hand up. "No, no. That's quite okay. If I'm wrong, I'm wrong. I absolutely don't want you to dash away and tell the person who referred you that I was blatantly unkind. I normally am not unkind. I'm normally quite pleasant and supportive."

Mariah fought back a sigh when his grin made a single dimple on one side of his face. His gray eyes lit with amusement. All in all… he was quite handsome.

"Unkind?" John asked. "Is that a new way of saying you tried to hand me my balls over something some other guy did to you?"

"Yes, and you're a very wise man for understanding. Please accept that this is a rare, rare day in my otherwise drama-free life," Mariah answered.

"Sure. I promise I will never tell anyone you were unkind to me," John promised softly, grinning still.

"Good. I wish you'd change your mind then. If you stay and talk to me, I promise to do my best to find your perfect date."

Head down and grinning even wider, John shook his head as he walked to the door. He raised his gaze to meet hers as he prepared to leave.

"I bet you could find her easier than you know. Good day, Dr. Bates. Maybe we'll run into each other again. Maybe I'll find my balls and come back. Anything is possible."

Mariah chuckled and felt her face heat. Lord, what had she done now? "I'll be more gentle with you next time," she promised, shocked to hear the flirty statement escape her mouth.

Laughing for real, John exited. Mariah turned to go to her office and saw Della still staring at the door. "What are you pondering, Dr. Livingston? The fact that I screwed up with a potential client, or the fact that I just went nova on a man in front of you?"

Della shook her head. "Actually, I was wondering how in the space of five minutes you went from yelling at Detective Monroe to flirting with him. Also, I'm 99.9% confident he started the flirting part of the exchange with his balls comment. I feel like I should be taking notes, but I wouldn't know where to catalog what just happened."

Mariah waved a hand. "What you witnessed was two mistakes clearing up awkwardly. Detective Monroe was never going to let me help him find a woman. Which is just as well because I'm not sure I could have matched up a still working detective without advising the woman to run away as fast as her legs could move. It's oddly fortunate that I ran him off because now I don't have to worry about my conflict of interest. It was a fairly charming end to a less than charming problem."

Della chuckled. "I'm pretty sure that was a beginning, not any kind of end."

Rolling her eyes at her young assistant's dreamy gaze, Mariah headed back to her office.

SHOULD SHE TELL HER LAST CLIENT OF THE DAY THAT HIS ALLEGED uncle had come by to see her? No, of course not. What if the man hadn't revealed his intentions to his nephew? There was no reason to compound her professional sins.

Pushing away thoughts of the grinning John Monroe, whoever he really was, Mariah studied the man leaning forward in his seat. He sighed at nearly every picture he saw.

"Problem with my choices for you, Mr. McElroy?"

Elliston McElroy, a successful entrepreneur who made software apps for a living, didn't answer her question immediately. He lifted and held up his swiping finger briefly before returning to his task of looking through the women on the tablet she'd handed him.

According to his worksheet, Elliston was five-foot ten, but he carried himself like he was six-foot eight, a family trait probably since the uncle was over six-foot tall. His close-cropped, light brown hair was gelled to stand straight up on top. The spiked hair, along with the tribal tattoos running down both forearms to his hands, created a European Soccer team look. Despite the faddishness, he pulled off the dress clothes he wore well. The sleeves of his well-made pressed cotton shirt were rolled casually to his elbows, no doubt to show off the tats. Mariah thought his thirty-two year old character was mostly revealed in the clear, blue-eyed gaze he turned her direction just before he spoke.

"Please call me Elliston. I can't handle the mister stuff. The women you picked for me are all very beautiful," he said at last.

Mariah shrugged. "We do mini-makeovers to help each client present their best for our catalogue. It helps that most work out and keep themselves maintained. I often tell male clients that we enhance female clients for presentation purposes only. Most do look a lot like their photos. I find people don't like physical surprises in dates."

Elliston sighed again.

"You're sighing very heavily, Elliston. What's wrong with them?" Mariah prompted.

His grin over her understanding was very arresting because his real masculine beauty showed up in it. Any woman would be thrilled to see that smile on his face every time she came into view. Elliston wasn't classically handsome with all those lean angles to his face, but he had that something special that made a woman want to stare at him until he snatched her up and kissed her senseless.

Now it was her turn to sigh. Mariah took her mild awareness of his maleness as a healthy sign in herself and a great sign for being able to find him someone.

Elliston slid the tablet back across the desk. "They're all my age or younger. They're like the women on all the dating sites. And I'm sure they're all very nice."

"They are," Mariah agreed. "I make sure of that."

Elliston nodded. "I guess I was hoping to find a little more maturity in my potential matches."

Mariah laughed before she could stop herself. She covered her mouth with her hand, but his narrowing gaze said she'd been caught indulging. The last thing she needed was to alienate a client with her oddball sense of humor. She was messing up as badly with Elliston as she had with his alleged uncle, John Monroe. She tamed her smile and cleared her throat.

"Am I to understand that you want me to find you someone who is older than you are?" Mariah asked to confirm.

Elliston nodded. "Yes. I think I do want that." He waved a hand at the tablet. "I've dated them already. They want a house, babies, and they get aggressive when they find out I have enough money to give that to them immediately. My perfect date is not that kind of woman. Mine is someone who just wants dinner and the pleasure of my company. That's harder to find than you might think. That's why I came to you."

Mariah nodded. "No, no. I quite believe you. However..." she paused for effect, "you need to know that mature women want things just as passionately as younger women. They just want different things than a house and babies. They want things like serious attention and utmost respect. How long is your attention span, Elliston? An older woman will demand you give her a lot of it. At the risk of being too blunt, that includes any time spent in bed."

Elliston favored her with his grin again. It really was one of his most appealing qualities. Mariah couldn't help but return it.

"I'm a great team player. I'm sure she and I can design a relationship that suits us both. The bed stuff is down the line anyway. Bed partners, like beautiful women, are easy to come by. Finding someone worth talking to is the bigger challenge."

Mariah chuckled softly. "Okay then. You've convinced me your request is sincere. Give me a couple of days to comb my database again. What's your *maturity* ceiling on age?"

He shrugged one shoulder. "I don't know. I'm pretty open-minded. What's the oldest woman in your database?"

Laughter again slipped right out of her mouth. If she wasn't so jaded, she might consider putting herself on Elliston's list. He was so… what was the word she searched for… *refreshing*? Yes, his attitude was refreshing.

"My oldest client is sixty-five and would not be a good match for you. She's a racing engineer who likes to go bungee jumping and zip lining through forests. She hates to read and watch TV. You two would never work. There would be no quiet dinners and pleasant conversations."

Elliston's answering laughter had that masculine grin permanently attaching itself to his face. "I don't know…" he teased.

Mariah shook her head. "I'll keep my recommendations for you to women under forty-five. That two decade mark is a hard dividing line. Even one decade can be a serious challenge."

"Challenge I can handle," Elliston said. "Being bored to death is my problem."

"No one I match you with will be boring," Mariah promised.

Elliston nodded. "How fast…" he paused and looked guilty. "I know this isn't like just drawing a random numbered person out of your data. But the fundraising gala is two weeks from now and…" he waved to the tablet. "I really don't want to have to take one of them. The place will be swarming with eligible bachelors from the tri-state. I'd like the woman I'm with to at least look like she's paying attention to me."

Insecurity, Mariah thought, as she nodded. It was something everyone struggled with until they met that one person who saw only them. Now it was her turn to sigh. Maybe she wasn't as jaded as she thought.

"I'm going to work on this today and tomorrow. Hopefully, I'll have some more choices for you by Friday."

"I don't mind any extra costs you have for the re-do. I just didn't know how to say what I wanted before. I should have been more open from the start," Elliston said.

"Yes. Open is good. I highly appreciate a man with an open mind and an open wallet," Mariah joked. "So let me get back to this and I'll get back to you as soon as I have some options."

3

"HERE. I MADE YOU SOME HOT TEA WITH CHAMOMILE. IT WON'T iron out those worry lines crossing your barely forty year old face, but it might settle down those jingling nerves of yours. You're muttering to yourself again, Mariah. I heard you all the way in the kitchen."

She lifted the mug from the serving tray and sipped. No dainty cups in her mother's household. "Thanks, Mom."

"You're welcome. Now when are you moving out? Someone as successful as you are shouldn't be consigned to living in this tiny patio home with me. I know Dan left you enough cash to buy another place. I mean... you're welcome to stay, but staying with me just makes it look like that selfish prick financially took you off at the knees."

Mariah snorted at the blunt comments and at her mother's swearing. People often thought she'd gotten her bluntness from her Air Force Colonel father. That could have been the case, but it wasn't. She'd gotten it from Georgia Bates, silver-haired smart-ass extraordinaire, and possibly the best mother on the planet.

"Andrew's getting ready to take the bar next year. Did you ever tell him what his bastard of a father did—or at least tried to do—to you?" Georgia asked.

"No," Mariah said, shaking her head. "And I don't intend to. I didn't tell Amanda either. With the baby coming, she doesn't need the stress. Randy's promotion came through. They're already having to move from Long Beach to Norfolk. Amanda is full up on things to worry about. The divorce was hard enough on her. She cries every time it comes up."

Georgia sniffed. "That's baby hormones. I know you raised her to be smarter about men. In my opinion, Dan's completely redefining what being an asshole means. Criminal charges. I can't believe he did that to the mother of his children. What's really criminal is that twenty-something blonde he's boffing these days."

"Mom, please… just let it go. God knows I have. The kids don't need to be part of Dan's divorce vendetta against me. For better or worse, he's still their father."

"It's been *for worse* since you left your marriage and that's all on him. I swear that's all I'm going to say about the matter. I'm just mad. Your heart wasn't the only one he broke, Mariah. You married him so young that Dan felt like my own son. But if he'd really been my child, I would have done a lot better job raising him. I'm almost glad Ted died before this happened. He'd have gone for Dan's balls."

Her mother's words instantly made her think of John's description of what her rant did to him. Maybe she'd been channeling her father that day. Mariah relaxed only when her mother patted her shoulder. Her father had died of a heart attack when she was a freshman in college. Her mother had grieved terribly for all the years it took her to get her PhD. Then one day her mother started living again. She'd been a terrific grandmother. She'd soon be a great-grandmother in every sense of that term. Not bad for a sharp, healthy woman in her early sixties who could out swear most men when she got angry.

"Bill was great. He practically handled it all for me. Everything got dismissed and no records will be kept of the charges. But I promise you Dan is the least of my problems at the moment. I have a couple of serious decisions to make, one of which has me stumped."

Georgia grunted. "Why? What's up? Is it anything you can discuss?"

Mariah laughed wryly. "It's no big secret, I guess. More and more young men are starting to ask for an older woman to date. This is not because they think older women are sexy or fun though. It's because they don't want to date a younger woman who wants the whole relationship package. They act like it's wrong for a woman of childbearing age to want marriage and babies. What is wrong with men these days?'

"Not a damn thing," Georgia said. "Women are the ones who've changed. A woman doesn't want to do the real work of shopping for the right guy any more. She picks one from one of those dating sites and then expects him to instantly step up to meet her relationship goals. What about genuine chemistry? What about taking the time to smile across the dinner table? It takes time and persistence, and maybe ten pounds of luck to find the right person. Men need time to figure things out way more than women do. Love, marriage, and family should not be a goal anyway. It's a special gift, not something to barter."

"Yes, Mom." Mariah answered simply because any complex answer would have extended the rant. "Got any friends near my age looking for the perfect man to date? Looks like I suddenly have openings for older women. Maybe I can offer them a discount to be listed."

Georgia thought for a moment. "I might. Let me think about

it. How about you list them for free and let the guy pick up the tab for it. In my day, men paid their way into a woman's heart."

"I'll see if my budget can afford it," Mariah promised.

When her mother left the room, she quietly sighed in relief and went back to looking for Elliston's perfect woman.

THE ONLY HALF-SUITABLE WOMAN IN HER DATABASE TURNED OUT to be forty-three, which was just over the decade mark she'd set for herself in her search. It didn't surprise her that Elliston approved Lynn's appearance and bio, even though the woman visibly looked older than him. They'd even met for coffee once. From that, they'd cemented tonight's date—a date where Mariah hovered in the background like a spying mother.

Good thing she had a legitimate reason to be there, at least as legitimate as every other person attending, because she too was a contributor. But this was not how the perfect dates she arranged were supposed to work. For one thing, she was not supposed to get directly involved. Or spy on them just because she was a tad concerned.

Either the chemistry was there for the couple or it wasn't. Her clients paid a considerable amount for her to do their searching. She charged a price to be listed and a price to be matched. Someone could pay the matching price or just hope Mariah eventually picked them. Males—true to their biological urges and their earning potential—seemed to order the matching more often since it was double the price of just being listed in the database.

However, there was one universal she'd seen in the year she'd been in business. Most clients wanted dates who were younger than them, or at least they wanted someone no more than their age, which was the root of her problem now. It wasn't what Elliston McElroy had asked for and she'd had a tough time sincerely believing someone his age wanted to spend time with someone so much older. Did those May men and December women sometimes work out? Sure, they did—out in the predatory wild of bars, singles groups, and online hookup apps. Sometimes those relationships did beat the odds against them and lasted. They just weren't something she wanted to base her business model on.

"Now I understand why my instincts told me to run like hell the other day. Do you always spy on your clients?"

Mariah closed her eyes briefly. What did it say about her that she still recognized his voice after two weeks had gone by. It said she'd been celibate too long. That's what it said.

Her divorce had been final for nearly a year, but Dan hadn't touched her for almost a year before that. He'd moved into another bedroom the moment she'd turned in her radio show resignation. She still made money off the syndication of the show, but what she was doing was helping her find her soul again.

"Detective Monroe."

"John," he corrected.

Mariah's mouth twisted into a reluctant smile. "Okay. How are you doing, John?"

He looked off at his nephew. "Did you really fix him up with someone old enough to be his mother?"

Something that had been blooming inside her suddenly wilted to dust. Had she really been nursing some fantasy about this man? Mariah looked across the room to Elliston and nodded her chin. "Elliston is such a nice man. Are you really his uncle?"

John turned to face her. "You didn't answer my question."

Mariah shrugged. "You didn't answer mine."

"Uncle John... you came."

John bent to offer his shorter nephew a man hug. He smirked as he met her gaze.

"Satisfied now?" he asked.

Mariah laughed. "Not really."

Elliston looked between them, a grin lighting his face. "You two know each other?"

"Not really," Mariah said again, enjoying the irritation lighting John's gaze. "We met as part of an ongoing investigation. Your uncle was so charming, I've decided not to hold the investigation against him. We were just making nice with each other when you walked over."

She raised a brow when John opened his mouth to deny her story, but it only took him two seconds to realize he'd have to confess the truth... or come up with a better lie.

"Touché," he said.

It was the oddest thing, but she just couldn't stop herself from laughing. Elliston and his uncle apparently brought out the wicked in her. She turned a bright smile towards her two clients. "I think everyone in Cincinnati and Northern Kentucky turned out for this. Let's hope they all made a large contribution."

Elliston nodded. "I knew the app I created for the fundraiser was going to get some traction, but I underestimated their interest in seeing my other work. I almost can't believe this. I should have at least put more business cards in my pockets."

Mariah dug in her purse and pulled out the three she'd taken from him the first time he'd come to see her. She carried them around because she'd liked him so much. "Here. You can replace them later. Don't miss any opportunities."

Snorting, John dug in his jacket before pulling out his wallet. He dug out three cards as well and handed them over to a now chuckling Elliston.

"Gee, thanks. Why couldn't you two be my parents? Mom and Dad didn't have any on them tonight," he said before turning to his date.

Elliston's tasteless joke deserved an eye roll from his date, but he seemed to be unaware that she was nearer her and John Monroe's age than his. Mariah winced a little at the pressure they'd all accidentally put on the woman now to top their support. Lynn Carson, an entrepreneur herself, merely smiled. She seemed unconcerned about any of it and pulled her phone out of a teeny, tiny sparkly gold shoulder purse resting against one curvy hip. She pulled Elliston's hand up, put one of his business cards in his palm, then took a picture of it.

Lynn smiled genuinely at him when he beamed at her. "There. Now you have something electronic to forward... and you can get them to give you their phone number this way. It's a twofer."

Mariah breathed out when Elliston turned that grin she found so appealing in her direction. "Thank you, Mariah. Tonight has truly been perfect," he said.

Mariah nodded—message received. Then Elliston and Lynn wandered off, leaving her alone again with John.

"How old is she?" John asked sharply. "You look younger than she does."

Mariah looked at him and made a zipper sign across her lips.

"Are you ever going to really talk to me?" he demanded.

"Sure. Just stop asking me questions about my clients. If you want to know more details about her, ask your nephew."

John grunted. "Yeah... okay. I get that."

"Good," Mariah said. "Now that I've seen what I came to see, I believe I'll be leaving. Can't say it was a pleasure to see you again, but it was just as interesting as the first time."

John stopped her with a hand on her arm. "Have coffee with me."

"Coffee? It's eight o'clock at night. My mother yells at me if I pace the house and keep her awake."

"You live with your mother?" John asked.

"I do now," Mariah said. "My ex got the house."

"How the hell did that happen?"

Mariah shrugged. "Something about him working to put me through college and how he was the primary reason I'd gotten wealthy, instead of it being my hard work like I'd believed. When calculated through divorce math, it apparently added up to an amount very similar to my half of our house."

"That's bullshit."

"That's divorce," Mariah corrected. "I'm going to buy another house. It's going to be a while though, unless my mother throws me out. I cramp her style. She's a party hound."

John's reluctant laughter over her comments made her chest warm with delight. There was nothing better to her than a man with a good sense of humor. But the rest of the package? Being a detective. Being a demanding nosy ass. God, it was like she was a magnet for men like Dan and him.

She caught him looking at Elliston, who put his hand on Lynn's arm to get her attention. He stayed attached to her while he listened to what she had to say in reply to his question.

And so it begins... Mariah reluctantly shook off her happier musings. "I could stand here and watch them all night, but only because they're having a good time together. Just so you can get your report straight, I don't normally chaperone."

"Now that sounded genuine," John said.

Mariah considered it for a moment. "It was. I like your nephew."

"So you do believe me."

Mariah laughed. "No. I believe Elliston. He's the one who cried uncle when he saw you."

John sighed. "Is it because of what I do for a living?"

"Is what?"

"You know what," John accused. "You putting me off."

"Off what?" Mariah asked.

"Liking you," John ground out. "Stop playing games. I know you can tell I'm interested."

"I don't date clients."

"But I'm not a client," John reminded her.

"I draw a different line," Mariah said carefully.

"Erase it," John ordered.

"And I just got divorced."

"From someone that took your house from you. Are you still pining?"

Mariah huffed. "No, I'm not pining. I'm just not interested. I'm… off men for a while… a good long while."

"How long?" John asked.

"Why are you pressing me so hard?" she asked, finding rationality in the blunt question.

"Because you're the most plain speaking woman I've ever met and I can see that extends to anyone you care about. Your ex is an idiot."

"My ex is Senior Detective Daniel Luray."

John wiped a hand over his eyes and said a pithy word or two under his breath.

"I take it you know him," Mariah observed, fascinated when John turned crimson again.

He finally nodded. "Yes. I'm working with him on a project."

Mariah shrugged. "Doesn't surprise me. At his level, nearly everyone interacts with Dan sooner or later. I'm sure he's already shared his suspicions about my business with you."

"Like most divorced men, Dan complains a lot," John said.

"Neither denying nor admitting," Mariah observed. "I feel a shift has taken place between us. I've morphed into a two headed Hydra right before your eyes."

"No," John denied. "That's not it."

"Bet it kicked that coffee idea to the curb though, didn't it?"

Reluctantly, John nodded. "It would make my work with him harder."

"Again... no surprise here," Mariah said.

"My project with him isn't going to last forever."

Mariah sighed and bowed her head. She lifted it only after several moments of debate about how honest to be.

"John... if I were a different female, I'd turn that coffee date into a Bourbon one, and then I'd seduce you. Not for your sake, but for mine. One—because I hate being celibate. Two—for the pleasure of knowing Dan was working alongside my new lover. Divorced women can be petty and vindictive, especially when they have an ex like I have. However, I'm not even going there in fantasy. Do you want to know why?"

"I'm riveted. Why?" John demanded.

"Because I like you as much as I like your nephew. And no one deserves to be treated badly. Watch your back, John. Dan is not the ethical straight-shooter he once was. I don't know what changed him, but something has. By the time we split, the once great father and husband was completely gone."

Needing to shut herself up, Mariah turned and walked away before she ended up answering that needy look John had given her when she'd confessed to liking him.

5

GEORGIA MOTIONED TO THE DINING TABLE. "OKAY, LADIES. FOOD'S all ready. Let's eat before Mariah gets home."

The women laughed as they filed down both sides of the table filling plates.

"I don't know if I can. I'm too nervous to eat. I can't believe I actually came here."

Reaching out, Georgia took her younger friend's arm and guided her to the table. On her best day, Jellica was forty-four going on twenty. It astounded her how few women had any real confidence in themselves. "You're going to be just fine. Eat now. It'll only be worse if you wait."

Georgia patted the woman's shoulder before pushing on it gently. It was always hard for her to deal with women friends who were afraid to make decisions, especially simple ones like eating.

"Why am I here, Georgia? I'm too old for this and the whole dating thing at our age is just ridiculous. I can't believe you talked me into this idiocy."

Georgia snickered as her head turned. "Quit complaining,

Trudy. You're getting free food you didn't have to cook yourself for once. Enjoy it while you can."

Chef Trudy Baxter frowned as she peered down at the buffet of nearly unidentifiable potluck dishes. "I like cooking just for myself."

"You do not," Georgia argued. "I eat with you at least three times a week."

"Only because I cook better than you do," Trudy argued.

"You're a famous chef, you eyelash batting widiot."

"Widiot—I love that. And I *was* a famous chef," Trudy corrected, frowning. "Now I'm just a retired restaurant owner with far too much free time on her hands."

"Stop bad mouthing yourself. You cook for friends and charities." Georgia snorted and shook her head. "Why am I wasting my breath arguing? Get a damn plate, Trudy. You're just here to keep Mariah from killing me. I was supposed to make her a list, not throw a potluck party. I got carried away."

"That must be a rare treat for a plodding harlot like you," Trudy answered, grinning. She looked at something yellow and then back to Georgia. "What did I tell you about using those recipes on the back of the corn can?"

"Will you just freaking eat," Georgia ordered sharply, pointing at the food.

Rolling her eyes, Trudy picked up a plate. "I can only imagine what your sex life must have been like with your husband. Was Ted into being bossed around?"

"Yes. We took turns at it," Georgia spat at her tormentor. She reached out, scooped up a helping of corn casserole, and plopped it onto Trudy's plate. "And yes, I made it from the recipe on the can. It's got fake cheese in it too."

Trudy glared at the offending glop of yellow nuggets. "Gross."

"So are your comments, you celibate sow."

Trudy's laugh over the insult happened just before the front door opened. Georgia winced and wiped her hands on her slacks. "She's early. Shit..."

"...is about to hit the proverbial Mariah fan," Trudy finished, putting her grinning attention on other dishes. "Do you really expect me to eat food I can't identify?"

Rolling her eyes, Georgia headed to talk to her daughter.

"Mom... you didn't," Mariah said wearily, sinking down on the guest room bed as she tried to take it in. She eyed the closed bedroom door, wishing she'd never come home tonight. "How many women did you invite?"

"Twenty-seven because I was sure some wouldn't show up."

Mariah rubbed her forehead. "Okay. So how many are actually here?"

"Thirty four or so. Word got around. No, make that thirty-three. Trudy doesn't count. She's not interested, but frankly, the woman needs to get laid. It's been like a decade for her."

Mariah's hand fell away. Her shock was now complete. What kind of business did her mother think she was running? She made it sound as bad as Dan did. "Mom, I'm not running a service to get women laid."

Georgia waved her hand. "You're so sensitive. That's not what I meant, Mariah."

"Well, what exactly did you mean?" Mariah demanded, irritation making her tone sharp.

She rose not waiting for an answer to her question. Logically, she knew her mother had been trying to help, but now what was she supposed to do with all those needy, and obviously desperate, women? Client acceptance was a rigorous process for her. This was all her fault for telling her fix-it mother about a shortage she wasn't even sure she wanted to fill.

Mariah groaned softly as her gaze took in the claustrophobic dimensions of the small bedroom. She really needed to find her own place where she could vent to the walls instead of to a woman who couldn't stop herself from over-fixing everything around her.

"I never realized how many unattached females I knew over the age of forty until you asked that question. Look at the bright side… at least there's food," Georgia offered as a penance. "Everyone who came brought a potluck dish. Some of it's even good enough to eat."

Mariah laughed only because angry swearing was a habit she could have all too easily picked up living under a roof again with Georgia Bates, military wife. She raised a hand instead, giving in ungracefully, because what else could she do? The women were here already.

"Fine. I'll be out there in ten minutes. But just know that I may not accept any of them. I'm not promising anyone anything."

Georgia shrugged. "Fine. I never promised them anything either."

"Good," Mariah said. "Because my male clients, even though some do want to date older women, have certain criteria for their matches. They expect successful, educated partners—not lonely housewives looking for boredom relief."

Georgia fisted her hands on her hips. "I think what they want is the same thing every man wants. They're just playing your expensive game to get you to do their hard work for them. Seems a little bit lazy to me, but I guess those twenty plus weddings prove you're doing something right."

"Mother…" Mariah warned, using the formality she knew her mother hated.

"Stop worrying. I knew better than to raise their hopes."

"Mother…" Mariah said softer. "This is not the way things are done."

"Well, it's a good thing then that we'll at least get food out of it. I put everyone in the Florida room so you could look at them in the daylight. Not a speck of foundation on any that I could tell so all the lines and wrinkles ought to be obvious. It shouldn't be hard to judge which ones will make a good enough high class showing."

"Mother…" Mariah said again, this time too exasperated to be stern.

"Don't forget to grab a plate on your way," Georgia ordered, opening the bedroom door and sliding out of it.

It surprised both her and her mother when Mariah actually came up with a list of eight potential women from the potluck attendees. They chatted about the women as they put plastic wrap over all the food worth keeping.

"Trudy's on my list. She's actually more like my typical female client. Maybe she's not into real dating at the moment, but I bet she wouldn't mind a few outings just for fun. Some of my clients just want an occasional companion with poise. Tell me more about Ann Lynx, though. She looks great for her age and didn't reek of desperation either."

Georgia stopped wrapping to think. "Ann's a long-time widow. Her nest is truly empty now that her son's getting married. I know I told you about her. Her daughter got busted up serving in the Marines. Girl came home and ended up marrying her childhood sweetheart. She was gone for over eight years. I'm surprised Nicholas North never came to see you."

"Nicholas North? Wow. He's from old money," Mariah said.

Georgia nodded. "Ann says he's a very good man who loves her daughter madly. That's better than money."

Mariah shrugged. "Dan and I certainly didn't marry for money. We were both in school."

"No, you didn't, but I sometimes wonder now about Dan's motives. You gave him a cushy lifestyle he would never have achieved on his own."

"Mom… we didn't break up over money. People fall out of love all the time."

"And some—like you—get pushed out of it," Georgia replied.

Mariah rolled her eyes, definitely not wanting to cover that ground again, even if she did still sometimes wonder what happened to her former relationship. Everything was great until one day it simply wasn't anymore.

"Back to the women who came tonight. Do you think Ann is really interested in finding someone new?"

"No."

Mariah laughed. Her mother was blunt to the point of conversational pain. "Why do you say that? You told me everyone who came here was interested."

Georgia turned and dug some plastic containers out of a nearby cabinet. "Oh, Ann's interested, but not necessarily in anything real. She came because Trudy and I made her. Ann's a happy widow, but her children are pressuring her to date. I think you represent a way she can make enough of a show of fake dating to keep her children off her back. All she has to do is tell them she's using a service."

Mariah frowned as she considered that info. Ann's lack of interest wouldn't work well with a male client wanting a real relationship. Usually she had the opposite problem with people wanting more than she could or anyone else could deliver.

"Do you feel like I ever pressure you to date?" Mariah asked, relieved when her mother laughed.

"No and I would never let you," she said firmly. "Not all mother-child relationships are as honest as ours though."

Mariah nodded as she wrapped the last dish. "Children just want their parents to be happy."

Georgia nodded. "Happiness doesn't always have to involve marriage and a man. Happy at my age can mean a lot of things. Ann's only in her early 50s. I can't speak for women her age. I lost your father then."

Mariah stopped and looked at her mother. "Do you still miss him?"

Georgia stopped spooning leftovers to think about it. "Not as much as I used to. He was a royal pain to live with after he retired. I do miss the sex, though. It was the glue that made the rough patches worth it between us. I always, always looked forward to that man coming home to me."

Mariah laughed and hung her head. She groaned a little. "Glad to hear Dad was a stud."

"Are you not dating because I'm not?" Georgia asked, the thought just occurring to her.

Mariah's head came flying up. "Of course not," she denied. "Because of Dan I hate men right now. This is not a good attitude to have when you want to date. I'm hoping it's a phase that will pass. I miss the sex too."

"Physician, heal thyself…" Georgia quoted.

Mariah snorted over the quote. "Except I'm not a physician. Nor apparently was I an expert at choosing a life partner either. My life has gotten very ironic given what I'm trying to do for a living."

Georgia fisted a hand on her hip. "Don't let Daniel Luray

become your standard for men. If I ever found a man I thought would be as good in bed as your father, I'd at least give him a go to see. The only reason that's likely never going to happen is that I'm not looking. That's both my fault and my decision. It doesn't mean there aren't any good men out there. You know it's all relative, Mariah. You can decide to be divorced and bitter, or you can decide to open up again. Either way will be no one's call, but yours. I know he had his own bedroom well over a year before the actual divorce. You're too young to go without that long."

Mariah chuckled and gave her mother a real smile. "I have a doctorate and am still only half as smart as you. How did you get that way? Tell me the truth."

"I said your father was good in bed," Georgia admitted. "I didn't say he was easy to live with outside of it. Military men are a lifelong education money can't buy. I was secretly glad when you married a civilian… or at least I was until Dan turned into a greedy bastard."

"You never told me that before… I mean about being glad I didn't marry someone in the military."

Georgia shrugged. "I was happy my grandchildren wouldn't be moving every three years. Ted and I had a good life, and we did the best by you kids as we could, but it wasn't always easy. Based on how exhausted I was by the time you hit college, I decided being settled in one place for most of your life was better."

"Yet you didn't blink when Amanda married Randy."

"They were high school sweethearts. That's a whole different matter. She loved him and he loved her. You didn't blink either."

Mariah sighed. "For the same reasons. Because she loved him… and he loved her. I was only worried because I didn't want my divorce to affect their belief that love was worth…"

She stopped and looked at her very smart mother. "Love. That's why it works or doesn't. When I married Dan, we worked."

Georgia lifted her hands.

Mariah walked around the bar and hugged her mother. "I'll try to remember to let love in if it shows up a second time in my life. Will you?"

She laughed when her mother's only answer was a long, exasperated sigh.

— **www.donnamcdonaldauthor.com** —

OTHER BOOKS BY THIS AUTHOR

Art Of Love Series
Carved In Stone
Created In Fire
Captured In Ink
Commissioned In White
Covered In Paint

The Perfect Date Series
Never Is A Very Long Time
Never Say Never
Never A Dull Moment
Never Ever Satisfied
Never Be Her Hero
Never Try To Explain
Never Look Back
More Coming Soon…

Never Too Late Series
Dating A Cougar

Dating Dr. Notorious
Dating A Saint
Dating A Metro Man
Dating A Silver Fox
Dating A Cougar II
Dating A Pro

Non-Series Books
The Wrong Todd
SEALed For Life
A Secret Dare
Saving Santa
Mistletoe Madness
No ELFing Way

Visit Donna's website to see more books.

ABOUT THE AUTHOR

DONNA MCDONALD

Donna McDonald published her first romance novel in March of 2011. Sixty plus novels later, she admits to living her own happily ever after as a full-time author. Her work spans several genres, such as contemporary romance, paranormal, and science fiction. Humor is the most common element in all her writing. Addicted to making readers laugh, she includes a good dose of romantic comedy in every book.

How To Connect With Donna…
www.donnamcdonaldauthor.com
email@donnamcdonaldauthor.com

facebook.com/donnamcdonaldauthor

twitter.com/donnamcdonald13

instagram.com/donnamcdonald13